CW00933242

The Eaten Heart

GIOVANNI BOCCACCIO

The Eaten Heart:
Unlikely Tales of Love

Translated by G. H. McWILLIAM

GREAT LOVES

To Vittore Branca
Primus studiorum dux

PENGUIN BOOKS

Published by the Penguin Group
Penguin Books Ltd, 80 Strand, London WC2R 0RL, England
Penguin Group (USA) Inc., 375 Hudson Street, New York, New York 10014, USA
Penguin Group (Canada), 90 Eglinton Avenue East, Suite 700, Toronto, Ontario, Canada M4P 2Y3
(a division of Pearson Penguin Canada Inc.)
Penguin Ireland, 25 St Stephen's Green, Dublin 2, Ireland
(a division of Penguin Books Ltd)
Penguin Group (Australia), 250 Camberwell Road, Camberwell, Victoria 3124, Australia
(a division of Pearson Australia Group Pty Ltd)
Penguin Books India Pvt Ltd, 11 Community Centre, Panchsheel Park, New Delhi – 110 017, India
Penguin Group (NZ), 67 Apollo Drive, Rosedale, North Shore 0632, New Zealand
(a division of Pearson New Zealand Ltd)
Penguin Books (South Africa) (Pty) Ltd, 24 Sturdee Avenue,
Rosebank, Johannesburg 2196, South Africa

Penguin Books Ltd, Registered Offices: 80 Strand, London WC2R 0RL, England

www.penguin.com

This translation first published 1972
Revised translation published 1995
This selection published in Penguin Books 2007
1

Copyright © G. H. McWilliam, 1972, 1995
All rights reserved

Typeset by Rowland Phototypesetting Ltd, Bury St Edmunds, Suffolk
Printed in England by Clays Ltd, St Ives plc

Except in the United States of America, this book is sold subject
to the condition that it shall not, by way of trade or otherwise, be lent,
re-sold, hired out, or otherwise circulated without the publisher's
prior consent in any form of binding or cover other than that in
which it is published and without a similar condition including this
condition being imposed on the subsequent purchaser

978-0-141-03278-8

Contents

1. Sowing the Seeds of Love   1
2. Love Wanders in the Night   12
3. Animal Passions   19
4. All Cats are Grey in the Dark   31
5. To Catch a Nightingale   39
6. Oh, to be a Virgin   48
7. Thorns of Desire   80
8. Head in the Herbs   95
9. Poor Man's Poison   101
10. The Loving Corpse   107
11. The Eaten Heart   116

Giovanni Boccaccio (1313–1375), a Florentine by birth, was a friend and correspondent of Petrarch and an important Renaissance humanist. Although he was initially apprenticed to the banking trade, and then to the study of canon law, Boccaccio later gave up his studies and devoted his time instead to literature. He moved to Naples in 1327, where he fathered two illegitimate children and also wrote his *Filostrato*, (the source for Chaucer's *Troilus and Criseyde)*, *Teseida* and *Filocolo*. Boccaccio began work on the *Decameron*, where the stories in this collection come from, around 1349. Comprising a hundred tales, the *Decameron* is told by ten Florentines who have fled their plague-ridden city and are entertaining each other as they take refuge in the countryside. It is best known for its bawdy tales of love, appearing in all its possibilities from the erotic to the tragic.

Sowing the Seeds of Love

There are a great many men and women who are so dense as to be firmly convinced that when a girl takes the white veil and dons the black cowl, she ceases to be a woman or to experience feminine longings, as though the very act of making her a nun had caused her to turn into stone. And if they should happen to hear of anything to suggest that their conviction is ill-founded, they become quite distressed, as though some enormous and diabolical evil had been perpetrated against Nature. It never enters their heads for a moment, possibly because they have no wish to face facts, that they themselves are continually dissatisfied even though they enjoy full liberty to do as they please, or that idleness and solitude are such powerful stimulants. Again, there are likewise many people who are firmly convinced that digging and hoeing and coarse food and hardy living remove all lustful desires from those who work on the land, and greatly impair their intelligence and powers of perception. [. . .], I would like to tell you a little tale, [. . .], which will show you quite clearly that all these people are sadly mistaken in their convictions.

In this rural region of ours, there was and still is a nunnery, greatly renowned for its holiness, which I shall refrain from naming for fear of doing the slightest harm to its reputation. At this convent, not long ago, at a time when it housed no more than eight nuns and an abbess, all of them young, there was a worthy little man whose job it was to look after a very beautiful garden of theirs. And one day, being dissatisfied with his remuneration, he settled up with the nuns' steward and returned to his native village of Lamporecchio.

On his return, he was warmly welcomed by several of the villagers, among them a young labourer, a big, strong fellow called Masetto, who, considering that he was of peasant stock, possessed a remarkably handsome physique and agreeable features. Since the good man, whose name was Nuto, had been away from the village for some little time, Masetto wanted to know where he had been, and when he learned that Nuto had been living at a convent, he questioned him about his duties there.

'I tended a fine, big garden of theirs,' Nuto replied, 'in addition to which, I sometimes used to go and collect firewood, or I would fetch water and do various other little jobs of that sort. But the nuns gave me such a paltry wage that it was barely sufficient to pay for my shoe-leather. Besides, they are all young and they seem to me to have the devil in them, because whatever you do, it is impossible to please them. Sometimes, in fact, I would be working in the garden when one of them would order me to do one thing, another would tell me to do something else, and yet another would snatch the very hoe from my hands, and tell me I was doing things the wrong way. They used to pester me to such an extent that occasionally I would down tools and march straight out of the garden. So that eventually, what with one thing and another, I decided I'd had enough of the place and came away altogether. Just as I was leaving, their steward asked me whether I knew of anyone who could take the job on, and I promised to send somebody along, provided I could find the right man, but you won't catch me sending him anybody, not unless God has provided the fellow with the strength and patience of an ox.'

As he listened, Masetto experienced such a longing to go and stay with these nuns that his whole body tingled with excitement, for it was clear from what he had heard that he should be able to achieve what he had in mind. Realizing, however, that he would get nowhere by revealing his intentions to Nuto, he replied:

'How right you were to come away from the place! What sort of a life can any man lead when he's surrounded by a lot of women? He might as well be living with a pack of devils. Why, six times out of seven they don't even know their own minds.'

But when they had finished talking, Masetto began to consider what steps he ought to take so that he could go and stay with them. Knowing himself to be perfectly capable of carrying out the duties mentioned by Nuto, he had no worries about losing the job on that particular score, but he was afraid lest he should be turned down because of his youth and his unusually attractive appearance. And so, having rejected a number of other possible expedients, he eventually thought to himself: 'The convent is a long way off, and there's nobody there who knows me. If I can pretend to be dumb, they'll take me on for sure.' Clinging firmly to this conjecture, he therefore dressed himself in pauper's rags and slung an axe over his shoulder, and without telling anyone where he was going, he set out for the convent. On his arrival, he wandered into the courtyard, where as luck would have it he came across the steward, and with the aid of gestures such as dumb people use, he conveyed the impression that he was begging for something to eat, in return for which he would attend to any wood-chopping that needed to be done.

The steward gladly provided him with something to eat, after which he presented him with a pile of logs that Nuto had been unable to chop. Being very powerful, Masetto made short work of the whole consignment, and then the steward, who was on his way to the wood, took Masetto with him and got him to fell some timber. He then provided Masetto with an ass, and gave him to understand by the use of sign-language that he was to take the timber back to the convent.

The fellow carried out his instructions so efficiently that the steward retained his services for a few more days, getting him to tackle various jobs that needed to be done about the place. One day, the Abbess herself happened to catch sight of him, and she asked the steward who he was.

'The man is a poor deaf-mute, ma'am, who came here one day begging for alms,' said the steward. 'I saw to it that he was well fed, and set him to work on various tasks that needed to be done. If he turns out to be good at gardening, and wants to stay, I reckon we would do well out of it, because we certainly need a gardener, and this is a strong fellow who will always do as he's told. Besides, you wouldn't need to worry about his giving any cheek to these young ladies of yours.'

'I do believe you're right,' said the Abbess. 'Find out whether he knows what to do, and make every effort to hold on to him. Provide him with a pair of shoes and an old hood, wheedle him, pay him a few compliments, and give him plenty to eat.'

The steward agreed to carry out her instructions, but Masetto was not far away, pretending to sweep the courtyard, and he had overheard their whole conversation. 'Once you put me inside that garden of yours,' he said to himself, gleefully, 'I'll tend it better than it's ever been tended before.'

Now, when the steward had discovered what an excellent gardener he was, he gestured to Masetto, asking him whether he would like to stay there, and the latter made signs to indicate that he was willing to do whatever the steward wanted. The steward therefore took him on to the staff, ordered him to look after the garden, and showed him what he was to do, after which he went away in order to attend to the other affairs of the convent, leaving him there by himself. Gradually, as the days passed and Masetto worked steadily away, the nuns started teasing and annoying him, which is the way people frequently behave with deaf-mutes, and they came out with the foulest language imaginable, thinking that he was unable to hear them. Moreover, the Abbess, who was possibly under the impression that he had lost his tail as well as his tongue, took little or no notice of all this.

Now one day, when Masetto happened to be taking a rest after a spell of strenuous work, he was approached by two very young nuns who were out walking in the garden. Since he gave them the impression that he was asleep, they began to stare at him, and the bolder of the two said to her companion:

'If I could be sure that you would keep it a secret, I would tell you about an idea that has often crossed my mind, and one that might well work out to our mutual benefit.'

'Do tell me,' replied the other. 'You can be quite certain that I shan't talk about it to anyone.'

The bold one began to speak more plainly.

'I wonder,' she said, 'whether you have ever considered what a strict life we have to lead, and how the only men who ever dare set foot in this place are the steward, who is elderly, and this dumb gardener of ours. Yet I have often heard it said, by several of the ladies who have come to visit us, that all other pleasures in the world are mere trifles by comparison with the one experienced by a woman when she goes with a man. I have thus been thinking, since I have nobody else to hand, that I would like to discover with the aid of this dumb fellow whether they are telling the truth. As it happens, there couldn't be a better man for the purpose, because even if he wanted to let the cat out of the bag, he wouldn't be able to. He wouldn't even know how to explain, for you can see for yourself what a mentally retarded, dim-witted hulk of a youth the fellow is. I would be glad to know what you think of the idea.'

'Dear me!' said the other. 'Don't you realize that we have promised God to preserve our virginity?'

'Pah!' she said. 'We are constantly making Him promises that we never keep! What does it matter if we fail to keep this one? He can always find other girls to preserve their virginity for Him.'

'But what if we become pregnant?' said her companion. 'What's going to happen then?'

'You're beginning to worry about things before they've even happened. We can cross that bridge if and when we come to it. There'll be scores of different ways to keep it a secret, provided we control our own tongues.'

'Very well, then,' said the other, who was already more eager than the first to discover what sort of stuff a man was made of. 'How do we set about it?'

'As you see,' she replied, 'it is getting on for nones, and I expect all our companions are asleep. Let's make sure there's nobody else in the garden. And then, if the coast is clear, all we have to do is to take him by the hand and steer him across to that hut over there, where he shelters from the rain. Then one of us can go inside with him while the other keeps watch. He's such a born idiot that he'll do whatever we suggest.'

Masetto heard the whole of this conversation, and since he was quite willing to obey, the only thing he was waiting for now was for one of them to come and fetch him. The two nuns had a good look round, and having made certain that they could not be observed, the one who had done all the talking went over to Masetto and woke him up, whereupon he sprang instantly to his feet. She then took him by the hand, making alluring gestures to which he responded with big broad, imbecilic grins, and led him into the hut, where Masetto needed very little coaxing to do her bidding. Having got what she wanted, she loyally made way for her companion, and Masetto, continuing to act the simpleton, did as he was asked. Before the time came for them to leave, they had each made repeated trials of the dumb fellow's riding ability, and later on, when they were busily swapping tales about it all, they agreed that it was every bit as pleasant an experience as they had been led to believe, indeed more so. And from then on, whenever the opportunity arose, they whiled away many a pleasant hour in the dumb fellow's arms.

One day, however, a companion of theirs happened to look out from the window of her cell, saw the goings-on, and drew the attention of two others to what was afoot. Having talked the matter over between themselves, they at first decided to report the pair to the Abbess. But then they changed their minds, and by common agreement with the other two, they took up shares in Masetto's holding. And because of various indiscretions, these five were subsequently joined by the remaining three, one after the other.

Finally, the Abbess, who was still unaware of all this, was taking a stroll one very hot day in the garden, all by herself, when she came across Masetto stretched out fast asleep in the shade of an almond-tree. Too much riding by night had left him with very little strength for the day's labours, and so there he lay, with his clothes ruffled up in front by the wind, leaving him all exposed. Finding herself alone, the lady stood with her eyes riveted to this spectacle, and she was seized by the same craving to which her young charges had already succumbed. So, having roused Masetto, she led him away to her room, where she kept him for several days, thus provoking bitter complaints from the nuns over the fact that the handyman had suspended work in the garden. Before sending him back to his own quarters, she repeatedly savoured the one pleasure for which she had always reserved her most fierce disapproval, and from then on she demanded regular supplementary allocations, amounting to considerably more than her fair share.

Eventually, Masetto, being unable to cope with all their demands, decided that by continuing to be dumb any longer he might do himself some serious injury. And so one night, when he was with the Abbess, he untied his tongue and began to talk.

'I have always been given to understand, ma'am,' he said, 'that whereas a single cock is quite sufficient for ten hens, ten men are hard put to satisfy one woman, and yet here am I with nine of them on my plate. I can't endure it any longer, not at any price, and as a matter of fact I've been on the go so much that I'm no longer capable of delivering the goods. So you'll either have to bid me farewell or come to some sort of an arrangement.'

When she heard him speak, the lady was utterly amazed, for she had always believed him to be dumb.

'What is all this?' she said. 'I thought you were supposed to be dumb.'

'That's right, ma'am, I was,' said Masetto, 'but I wasn't born dumb. It was owing to an illness that I lost the power of speech, and, praise be to God, I've recovered it this very night.'

The lady believed him implicitly, and asked him what he had meant when he had talked about having nine on his plate. Masetto explained how things stood, and when the Abbess heard, she realized that every single one of the nuns possessed sharper wits than her own. Being of a tactful disposition, she decided there and then that rather than allow Masetto to go away and spread tales concerning the convent, she would come to some arrangement with her nuns in regard to the matter.

Their old steward had died a few days previously. And so, with Masetto's consent, they unanimously decided, now that they all knew what the others had been doing, to persuade the people living in the neighbourhood that after a prolonged period of speechlessness, his ability to talk had been miraculously restored by the nuns' prayers and the virtues of the saint after whom the convent was named, and they appointed him their new steward. They divided up his various functions among themselves in such a way that he was able to do them all justice. And although he fathered quite a number of nunlets and monklets, it was all arranged so discreetly that nothing leaked out until after the death of the Abbess, by which time Masetto was getting on in years and simply wanted to retire to his village on a fat pension. Once his wishes became known, they were readily granted.

Thus it was that Masetto, now an elderly and prosperous father who was spared the bother of feeding his children and the expense of their upbringing, returned to the place from which he had set out with an axe on his shoulder, having had the sense to employ his youth to good advantage. And this, he maintained, was the way that Christ treated anyone who set a pair of horns on His crown.

Love Wanders in the Night

Not long ago, there lived in the valley of the Mugnone a worthy man who earned an honest penny by supplying food and drink to wayfarers; and although he was poor, and his house was tiny, he would from time to time, in cases of urgent need, offer them a night's lodging, but only if they happened to be people he knew.

Now, this man had a most attractive wife, who had borne him two children, the first being a charming and beautiful girl of about fifteen or sixteen, as yet unmarried, whilst the second was an infant, not yet twelve months old, who was still being nursed at his mother's breast.

The daughter had caught the eye of a lively and handsome young Florentine gentleman who used to spend much of his time in the countryside, and he fell passionately in love with her. Nor was it long before the girl, being highly flattered to have won the affection of so noble a youth, which she strove hard to retain by displaying the greatest affability towards him, fell in love with him. And neither of the pair would have hesitated to consummate their love, but for the fact that Pinuccio (for such was the young man's name) was not prepared to expose the girl or himself to censure.

At length however, his ardour growing daily more

intense, Pinuccio was seized with a longing to consort with her, come what may, and it occurred to him that he must find some excuse for lodging with her father overnight, since, being conversant with the layout of the premises, he had good reason to think that he and the girl could be together without anyone ever being any the wiser. And no sooner did this idea enter his head than he promptly took steps to carry it into effect.

Late one afternoon, he and a trusted companion of his called Adriano, who knew of his love for the girl, hired a couple of pack-horses, and having laden them with a pair of saddlebags, filled probably with straw, they set forth from Florence; and after riding round in a wide circle they came to the valley of the Mugnone, some time after nightfall. They then wheeled their horses round to make it look as though they were returning from Romagna, rode up to the cottage of our worthy friend, and knocked at the door. And since the man was well acquainted with both Pinuccio and his companion, he immediately came down to let them in.

'You'll have to put us up for the night,' said Pinuccio. 'We had intended to reach Florence before dark, but as you can see, we've made such slow progress that this is as far as we've come, and it's too late to enter the city at this hour.'

'My dear Pinuccio,' replied the host, 'as you know, I can't exactly offer you a princely sort of lodging. But no matter: since night has fallen and you've nowhere else to go, I shall be glad to put you up as best I can.'

So the two young men dismounted, and having seen that their nags were comfortably stabled, they went into the house, where, since they had brought plenty to eat with them, they made a hearty supper along with their host. Now, their host had only one bedroom, which was very tiny, and into this he had crammed three small beds, leaving so little space that it was almost impossible to move between them. Two of the beds stood alongside one of the bedroom walls, whilst the third was against the wall on the opposite side of the room; and having seen that the least uncomfortable of the three was made ready for his guests, the host invited them to sleep in that for the night. Shortly afterwards, when they appeared to be asleep, though in reality they were wide awake, he settled his daughter in one of the other two beds, whilst he and his wife got into the third; and beside the bed in which she was sleeping, his wife had placed the cradle containing her infant son.

Having made a mental note of all these arrangements, Pinuccio waited until he was sure that everyone was asleep, then quietly left his bed, stole across to the bed in which his lady-love was sleeping, and lay down beside her. Although she was somewhat alarmed, the girl received him joyously in her arms, and they then proceeded to take their fill of that sweet pleasure for which they yearned above all else.

Whilst Pinuccio and the girl were thus employed, a cat, somewhere in the house, happened to knock something over, causing the man's wife to wake up with a start. Being anxious to discover what it was, she got up and groped her way naked in the dark towards that part of the house from which the noise had come.

Meanwhile Adriano also happened to get up, not for the same reason, but in order to obey the call of nature, and as he was groping his way towards the door with this purpose in view, he came in contact with the cradle deposited there by the woman. Being unable to pass without moving it out of his way, he picked it up and set it down beside his own bed; and after doing what he had to do, he returned to his bed and forgot all about it.

Having discovered the cause of the noise and assured herself that nothing important had fallen, the woman swore at the cat, and, without bothering to light a lamp and explore the matter further, returned to the bedroom. Picking her way carefully through the darkness, she went straight to the bed where her husband was lying; but on finding no trace of the cradle, she said to herself: 'How stupid I am! What a fine thing to do! Heavens above, I was just about to step into the bed where my guests are sleeping.' So she walked a little further up the room, found the cradle, and got into bed beside Adriano, thinking him to be her husband.

On perceiving this, Adriano, who was still awake, gave her a most cordial reception; and without a murmur he tacked hard to windward over and over again, much to her delight and satisfaction.

This, then, was how matters stood when Pinuccio, who had gratified his longings to the full and was afraid of falling asleep in the young lady's arms, abandoned her so as to go back and sleep in his own bed. But on reaching the bed to find the cradle lying there, he moved on, thinking he had mistaken his host's bed for his own, and ended up by getting into bed with the host, who was awakened by his coming. And being under the impression that the man who lay beside him was Adriano, Pinuccio said:

'I swear to you that there was never anything so delicious as Niccolosa. By the body of God, no man ever had so much pleasure with any woman as I have been having with her. Since the time I left you, I assure you I've been to the bower of bliss half a dozen times at the very least.'

The host was not exactly pleased to hear Pinuccio's tidings, and having first of all asked himself what the devil the fellow was doing in his bed, he allowed his anger to get the better of his prudence, and exclaimed:

'What villainy is this, Pinuccio? I can't think why you should have played me so scurvy a trick, but by all that's holy, I shall pay you back for it.'

Now, Pinuccio was not the wisest of young men, and on perceiving his error, instead of doing all he could to remedy matters, he said:

'Pay me back? How? What could you do to me?'

Whereupon the host's wife, thinking she was with her husband, said to Adriano:

'Heavens! Just listen to the way those guests of ours are arguing with one another!'

Adriano laughed, and said:

'Let them get on with it, and to hell with them. They had far too much to drink last night.'

The woman had already thought she could detect the angry tones of her husband, and on hearing

Adriano's voice, she realized at once whose bed she was sharing. So being a person of some intelligence, she promptly got up without a word, seized her baby's cradle, and having picked her way across the room, which was in total darkness, she set the cradle down beside the bed in which her daughter was sleeping and scrambled in beside her. Then, pretending to have been aroused by the noise her husband was making, she called out to him and demanded to know what he was quarrelling with Pinuccio about. Whereupon her husband replied:

'Don't you hear what he says he has done to Niccolosa this night?'

'He's telling a pack of lies,' said the woman. 'He hasn't been anywhere near Niccolosa, for I've been lying beside her myself the whole time and I haven't managed to sleep a wink. You're a fool to take any notice of him. You men drink so much in the evening that you spend the night dreaming and wandering all over the place in your sleep, and imagine you've performed all sorts of miracles: it's a thousand pities you don't trip over and break your necks! What's Pinuccio doing there anyway? Why isn't he in his own bed?'

At which point, seeing how adroitly the woman was concealing both her own and her daughter's dishonour, Adriano came to her support by saying:

'How many times do I have to tell you, Pinuccio, not to wander about in the middle of the night? You'll land yourself in serious trouble one of these days, with this habit of walking in your sleep, and claiming to have actually done the fantastic things you dream about. Come back to bed, curse you!'

When he heard Adriano confirm what his wife had been saying, the host began to think that Pinuccio really had been dreaming after all; and seizing him by the shoulder, he shook him and yelled at him, saying:

'Wake up, Pinuccio! Go back to your own bed!'

Having taken all of this in, Pinuccio now began to thresh about as though he were dreaming again, causing his host to split his sides with laughter. But in the end, after a thorough shaking, he pretended to wake up; and calling to Adriano, he said:

'Why have you woken me up? Is it morning already?'

'Yes,' said Adriano. 'Come back here.'

Pinuccio kept up the pretence, showing every sign of being extremely drowsy, but in the end he left his host's side and staggered back to bed with Adriano. When they got up next morning, their host began to laugh and make fun of Pinuccio and his dreams. And so, amid a constant stream of merry banter, the two young men saddled and loaded their horses, and after drinking the health of their host, they remounted and rode back to Florence, feeling no less delighted with the manner than with the outcome of the night's activities.

From then on, Pinuccio discovered other ways of consorting with Niccolosa, who meanwhile assured her mother that he had certainly been dreaming. And thus the woman, who retained a vivid memory of Adriano's embraces, was left with the firm conviction that she alone had been awake on the night in question.

Animal Passions

Not so very long ago, there lived in Perugia a rich man called Pietro di Vinciolo, who, perhaps to pull the wool over the eyes of his fellow-citizens or to improve the low opinion they had of him, rather than because of any real wish to marry, took to himself a wife. But the unfortunate part about it, considering his own proclivities, was that he chose to marry a buxom young woman with red hair and a passionate nature, who would cheerfully have taken on a pair of husbands, let alone one, and now found herself wedded to a man whose heart was anywhere but in the right place.

Having in due course discovered how matters stood, his wife, seeing that she was a fair and lusty wench, blooming with health and vitality, was greatly upset about it, and every so often she gave him a piece of her mind, calling him the foulest names imaginable. She was miserable practically the whole time, but one day, realizing that if she went on like this her days might well be ended before her husband's ways were mended, she said to herself: 'Since this miserable sinner deserts me to go clogging through the dry, I'll get someone else to come aboard for the wet. I married the wretch, and brought him a good big dowry, because I knew he was a man and thought he was fond of the kind of thing that other men like, as is right and proper that they should. If I hadn't thought he was a man, I should never have married him. And if he found women so repugnant, why did he marry me in the first place, knowing me to be a woman? I'm not going to stand for it any longer, I have no desire to turn my back on the world, nor have I ever wanted to, otherwise I'd have gone into a nunnery; but if I have to rely on this fellow for my fun and games, the chances are that I'll go on waiting until I'm an old woman. And what good will it do me then, in my old age, to look back and complain about the way I wasted my youth, which this husband of mine teaches me all too well how to enjoy? He has shown me how to lead a pleasurable life, but whereas in his case the pleasure can only be condemned, in my own it will commend itself to all, for I shall simply be breaking the laws of marriage, whereas he is breaking those of Nature as well.'

These, then, were the wife's ideas, to which she doubtless gave further thought on other occasions, and in order to put them into effect, she made the acquaintance of an old bawd who to all outward appearances was as innocent as Saint Verdiana feeding the serpents, for she made a point of attending all the religious services clutching her rosary, and never stopped talking about the lives of the Fathers of the Church and the wounds of St Francis, so that nearly everyone regarded her as a saint. Choosing the right moment, the wife took her fully into her confidence, whereupon the old woman said:

'The Lord above, my daughter, who is omniscient, knows that you are very well advised, if only because you should never waste a moment of your youth, and the same goes for all other women. To anyone who's had experience of such matters, there's no sorrow to compare with that of having wasted your opportunities. After all, what the devil are we women fit for in our old age except to sit round the fire and stare at the ashes? No woman can know this better than I, or prove it to you more convincingly. Now that I am old, my heart bleeds when I look back and consider the opportunities I allowed to go to waste. Mind you, I didn't waste all of them – I wouldn't want you to think I was a half-wit – but all the same I didn't do as much as I should have done. And God knows what agony it is to see myself reduced now to this sorry state, and realize that if I wanted to light a fire, I couldn't find anyone to lend me a poker.

'With men it is different: they are born with a thousand other talents apart from this, and older men do a far better job than younger ones as a rule; but women exist for no other purpose than to do this and to bear children, which is why they are cherished and admired. If you doubt my words, there's one thing that ought to convince you, and that is that a woman's always ready for a man, but not vice-versa. What's more, one woman could exhaust many men, whereas many men can't exhaust one woman. And since this is the purpose for which we are born, I repeat that you are very well advised to pay your husband in his own coin, so that when you're an old woman your heart will have no cause for complaint against your flesh.

'You must help yourself to whatever you can grab in

this world, especially if you're a woman. It's far more important for women than for men to make the most of their opportunities, because when we're old, as you can see for yourself, neither our husbands nor any other man can bear the sight of us, and they bundle us off into the kitchen to tell stories to the cat, and count the pots and pans. And what's worse, they make up rhymes about us, such as "When she's twenty give her plenty. When she's a gammer, give her the hammer," and a lot of other sayings in the same strain.

'But I won't detain you any longer with my chit-chat. You've told me what you have in mind, and I can assure you right away that you couldn't have spoken to anyone in the world who was better able to help. There's no man so refined as to deter me from telling him what's required of him, nor is there any so raw and uncouth as to prevent me from softening him up and bending him to my will. So just point out the one you would like, and leave the rest to me. But one thing I would ask you to remember, my child, and that is to offer me some token of your esteem, for I'm a poor old woman, and from now on I want you to have a share in my indulgences and all the paternosters I recite, so that God may look with favour on the souls of your departed ones.'

Having said her piece, she came to an understanding with the young lady that if she should come across a certain young man who frequently passed through that part of the city, and of whom she was given a very full description, she would take all necessary steps. The young woman then handed over a joint of salted meat, and they took their leave of one another.

Within the space of a few days, the youth designated by the lady was ushered secretly into her apartments by the beldam, and thereafter, at frequent intervals, several others who had taken the young woman's fancy were similarly introduced to her. And although she was in constant fear of being discovered by her husband, she made the fullest possible use of her opportunities.

One evening, however, her husband having been invited to supper by a friend of his called Ercolano, the young woman commissioned the beldam to fetch her one of the prettiest and most agreeable youths in Perugia, and her instructions were duly carried out. But no sooner were she and the youth seated at the supper-table than her husband, Pietro, started clamouring at the door to be let in.

The woman was convinced, on hearing this, that her final hour had come. But all the same she wanted to conceal the youth if possible, and not having the presence of mind to hide him in some other part of the house, she persuaded him to crawl beneath a chicken-coop in the lean-to adjoining the room where they were dining, and threw a large sack over the top of it, which she had emptied of its contents earlier in the day. This done, she quickly let in her husband, to whom she said as he entered the house:

'You soon gobbled down that supper of yours.'

'We never ate a crumb of it,' replied Pietro.

'And why was that?' said his wife.

'I'll tell you why it was,' said Pietro. 'No sooner had Ercolano, his wife and myself taken our places at table than we heard someone sneezing, close beside where we

23

were sitting. We took no notice the first time it happened, or the second, but when the sneezing was repeated for the third, fourth and fifth times, and a good many more besides, we were all struck dumb with astonishment. Ercolano was in a bad mood anyway because his wife had kept us waiting for ages before opening the door to let us in, and he rounded on her almost choking with fury, saying: "What's the meaning of this? Who's doing all that sneezing?" He then got up from the table, and walked over to the stairs, beneath which there was an alcove boarded in with timber, such as people very often use for storing away bits and pieces when they're tidying up the house.

'As this was the place from which Ercolano thought the sneezes were coming, he opened a little door in the wainscoting, whereupon the whole room was suddenly filled with the most appalling smell of sulphur, though a little while before, when we caught a whiff of sulphur and complained about it, Ercolano's wife said: "It's because I was using sulphur earlier in the day to bleach my veils. I sprinkled it into a large bowl so that they would absorb the fumes, then placed it in the cupboard under the stairs, and it's still giving off a faint smell." After opening the little door and waiting for the fumes to die down a little, Ercolano peered inside and caught sight of the fellow who'd been doing all the sneezing, and was still sneezing his head off because of the sulphur. But if he'd stayed there much longer he would never have sneezed again, nor would he have done anything else for that matter.

'When he saw the man sitting there in the cupboard,

Ercolano turned to his wife and shouted: "Now I see, woman, why you kept us waiting so long at the door just now, without letting us in; but I'll make you pay for it, if it's the last thing I do." On hearing this, since it was perfectly obvious what she had been doing, his wife got up from the table without a word of explanation and took to her heels, and what became of her I have no idea. Not having noticed that his wife had fled, Ercolano called repeatedly on the man who was sneezing to come out, but the fellow was already on his last legs and couldn't be persuaded to budge. So Ercolano grabbed him by one of his feet, dragged him out, and ran for a knife in order to kill him, at which point, since I was afraid we would all be arrested, myself included, I leapt to my feet and saved him from being killed or coming to any harm. As I was defending him from Ercolano, my shouts brought several of the neighbours running to the scene, and they picked up the youth, who was no longer conscious, and carried him out of the house, but I've no idea where they took him. All this commotion put paid to our supper, so that, as I said, not only did I not gobble it down, but I never ate a crumb of it.'

On hearing this tale, his wife perceived that other women, even though their plans occasionally miscarried, were no less shrewd than herself, and she was strongly tempted to speak up in defence of Ercolano's wife. But thinking that by censuring another's misconduct she would cover up her own more successfully, she said:

'What a nice way to behave! What a fine, God-fearing specimen of womanhood! What a loyal and respectable spouse! Why, she had such an air of saintliness that she looked as if butter wouldn't melt in her mouth! But the worst part about it is that anyone as old as she is should be setting the young so fine an example. A curse upon the hour she was born! May the Devil take the wicked and deceitful hussy, for allowing herself to become the general butt and laughing-stock of all the women of this city! Not only has she thrown away her own good name, broken her marriage vows, and forfeited the respect of society, but she's had the audacity, after all he has done for her, to involve an excellent husband and venerable citizen in her disgrace, and all for the sake of some other man. So help me God, women of her kind should be shown no mercy; they ought to be done away with; they ought to be burnt alive and reduced to ashes.'

But at this point, recollecting that her lover was concealed beneath the chicken-coop in the very next room, she started coaxing Pietro to go to bed, saying it was getting late, whereupon Pietro, who had a greater urge to eat than to sleep, asked her whether there was any supper left over.

'Supper?' she replied. 'What would I be doing cooking supper, when you're not at home to eat it? Do you take me for the wife of Ercolano? Be off with you to bed, and give your stomach a rest, just for this once.'

Now, earlier that same evening, some of the labourers from Pietro's farm in the country had turned up at the house with a load of provisions, and had tethered their asses in a small stable adjoining the lean-to without bothering to water them. Being frantic with thirst, one of the asses, having broken its tether, had strayed from the stable and was roaming freely about the premises, sniffing in every nook and cranny to see if it could find any water. And in the course of its wanderings, it came and stood immediately beside the coop under which the young man lay hidden.

Since the young man was having to crouch on all fours, one of his hands was sticking out slightly from underneath the coop, and as luck would have it (or rather, to his great misfortune) the ass brought one of its hooves to rest on his fingers, causing him so much pain that he started to shriek at the top of his voice. Pietro, hearing this, was filled with astonishment, and, realizing that the noise was coming from somewhere inside the house, he rushed from the room to investigate. The youth was still howling, for the ass had not yet shifted its hoof from his fingers and was pressing firmly down upon him all the time. 'Who's there?' yelled Pietro as he ran to the coop, lifting it up to reveal the young man, who, apart from suffering considerable pain from having his fingers crushed beneath the hoof of the ass, was trembling with fear from head to foot in case Pietro should do him some serious injury.

Pietro recognized the young man as one he had long been pursuing for his own wicked ends, and demanded to know what he was doing there. But instead of answering his question, the youth pleaded with him for the love of God not to do him any harm.

'Get up,' said Pietro. 'There's no need to worry, I shan't do you any harm. Just tell me what you're doing here, and how you got in.'

The young man made a clean breast of the whole

thing, and Pietro, who was no less pleased with his discovery than his wife was filled with despair, took him by the hand and led him back into the room, where the woman was waiting for him in a state of indescribable terror. Pietro sat down, looked her squarely in the face, and said:

'When you were heaping abuse on Ercolano's wife just now, and saying that she ought to be burnt alive, and that she was giving women a bad name, why didn't you say the same things about yourself? And if you wanted to keep yourself out of it, what possessed you to say such things about her, when you knew full well that you were tarred with the same brush? The only reason you did it, of course, was because all you women are alike. You go out of your way to criticize other people's failings so as to cover up your own. Oh, how I wish that a fire would descend from Heaven and burn the whole revolting lot of you to ashes!'

On finding that all she had to contend with, in the first flush of his anger, was a string of verbal abuse, and noting how delighted he seemed to be holding such a good-looking boy by the hand, the wife plucked up courage and said:

'It doesn't surprise me in the least that you want a fire to descend from Heaven and burn us all to ashes, seeing that you're as fond of women as a dog is fond of a hiding, but by the Holy Cross of Jesus you'll not have your wish granted. However, now that you've raised the subject, I'd like to know what you're grumbling about. It's all very well for you to compare me to Ercolano's wife, but at least he gives that sanctimonious old trollop whatever she wants, and treats her as a wife should be treated, which is more than can be said for you. I grant you that you keep me well supplied with clothes and shoes, but you know very well how I fare for anything else, and how long it is since you last slept with me. And I'd rather go barefoot and dressed in rags, and have you treat me properly in bed, than have all those things to wear and a husband who never comes near me. For the plain truth is, Pietro, that I'm no different from other women, and I want the same that they are having. And if you won't let me have it, you can hardly blame me if I go and get it elsewhere. At least I do you the honour not to consort with stable-boys and riff-raff.'

Pietro saw that she could go on talking all night, and since he was not unduly interested in his wife, he said:

'Hold your tongue now, woman, and leave everything to me. Be so good as to see that we're supplied with something to eat. This young man looks as though he's had no more supper this evening than I have.'

'Of course he hasn't had any supper,' said his wife. 'We were no sooner seated at table than you had to come knocking at the door.'

'Run along, then,' said Pietro, 'and get us some supper, after which I'll arrange matters so that you won't have any further cause for complaint.'

On perceiving that her husband was so contented, the wife sprang to her feet and quickly relaid the table. And when the supper she had prepared was brought in, she and the youth and her degenerate husband made a merry meal of it together.

How exactly Pietro arranged matters, after supper, to

the mutual satisfaction of all three parties, I no longer remember. But I do know that the young man was found next morning wandering about the piazza, not exactly certain with which of the pair he had spent the greater part of the night, the wife or the husband. So my advice to you, dear ladies, is this, that you should always give back as much as you receive; and if you can't do it at once, bear it in mind till you can, so that what you lose on the swings, you gain on the roundabouts.

All Cats are Grey in the Dark

When Agilulf became King of the Lombards, he followed the example set by his predecessors and chose the city of Pavia, in Lombardy, as the seat of his kingdom. He had meanwhile married Theodelinda, who was the beautiful widow of the former Lombard king, Authari, and although she was a very intelligent and virtuous woman, she once had a most unfortunate experience with a suitor of hers. For during a period when the affairs of Lombardy, owing to the wise and resolute rule of this King Agilulf, were relatively calm and prosperous, one of the Queen's grooms, a man of exceedingly low birth, gifted out of all proportion to his very humble calling, who was as tall and handsome as the King himself, happened to fall hopelessly in love with his royal mistress.

Since his low station in life had not blinded him to the fact that this passion of his was thoroughly improper, he had the good sense not to breathe a word about it to anyone, nor did he even dare to cast tell-tale glances in the lady's direction. But although he was quite resigned to the fact that he would never win her favour, he could at least claim that his thoughts were directed towards a lofty goal. And being scorched all over by the flames of love, he outshone every one of his companions by the zealous manner in which he performed any trifling service that might conceivably bring pleasure to the Queen. Thus it came about that whenever the Queen was obliged to go out on horse-back, she preferred to ride the palfrey that was under his care, rather than any of the others. On these occasions, the fellow considered himself to be in his seventh heaven, and he would remain close beside her stirrup, almost swooning with joy whenever he was able simply to brush against the lady's clothes.

However, one frequently finds in affairs of this sort that the weakening of expectation goes hand in hand with a strengthening of the initial passion, and that is exactly what happened in the case of this poor groom. So much so, in fact, that having no glimmer of hope to sustain him, he found it increasingly difficult to keep his secret yearnings under control, and since he was unable to rid himself of his passion, he kept telling himself that he would have to die. In reflecting on the ways and the means, he was determined to die in such a manner that his motive, in other words his love for the Queen, would be inferred from the circumstances leading up to his death. And at the same time, he resolved that these circumstances should offer him an opportunity of trying his luck and seeing whether he could bring his desires either wholly or partially to fruition. Knowing that it would be quite futile to start either confiding in the Queen or writing letters to acquaint her with his love, he thought he would explore the possibility of entering her bed by means of a stratagem. He had already discovered that the King was not in the habit of invariably sleeping with her, and hence the one and only stratagem that might conceivably succeed was for him to find some way of impersonating the King so that he could approach her quarters and gain admittance to her bedchamber.

Accordingly, with the aim of discovering how the King was dressed and what procedure he followed when paying the Queen a visit, the groom concealed himself for several nights running in the King's palace, in a spacious hall situated between the respective royal bedchambers. And during one of these nocturnal vigils, he saw the King emerge from his room in an enormous cloak, with a flaming torch in one hand and a stick in the other. Walking over to the Queen's room, the King knocked once or twice on the door with his stick, whereupon he was instantly admitted and the torch was removed from his hand. Some time later, the King retired in like fashion to his own quarters, and the groom, who had been keeping a careful watch, decided that he too would have to adopt this same ritual. He therefore procured a torch and a stick, and a cloak similar to the one he had seen the King wearing, and having soaked himself thoroughly in a hot bath so that there should be no possibility of his giving offence to the Queen or arousing her suspicions by smelling of the stable, he transported these articles to the great hall and concealed himself in his usual place.

When he sensed that everyone was asleep, and that the time had finally come for him to gratify his longing or perish nobly in the attempt, he kindled a small flame with the aid of a flint and steel that he had brought along for the purpose, lit his torch, and, wrapping himself carefully up in the folds of the cloak, walked over to the door of the bedchamber and knocked twice with his stick. The door was opened by a chambermaid, still half asleep, who took the light and put it aside, whereupon without uttering a sound he stepped inside the curtain, divested himself of his cloak, and clambered into the bed where the Queen was sleeping. Knowing that the King, whenever he was angry about anything, was in the habit of refusing all discourse, he drew the Queen lustfully into his arms with a show of gruff impatience, and without a single word passing between them, he repeatedly made her carnal acquaintance. He was most reluctant to depart, but nevertheless he eventually arose, fearing lest by over-staying his welcome the delight he had experienced should be turned into sorrow, and having donned his cloak and retrieved his torch, he stole wordlessly away and returned as swiftly as possible to his own bed.

He could hardly have reached his destination when, to the Queen's utter amazement, the King himself turned up in her room, climbed into bed, and offered her a cheerful greeting.

'Heavens!' she said, emboldened to speak by his affable manner. 'Whatever has come over you tonight, my lord? You no sooner leave me, after enjoying me more passionately than usual, than you come back and start all over again! Do take care of your health!'

On hearing these words, the King immediately came to the conclusion that the Queen had been taken in by an outward resemblance to his own physique and manner. But he was a wise man, and since neither the

Queen nor anybody else appeared to have noticed the deception, he had no hesitation in deciding to keep his own counsel. Many a stupid man would have reacted differently, and exclaimed: 'It was not I. Who was the man who was here? What happened? Who was it who came?' But this would only have led to complications, upsetting the lady when she was blameless and sowing the seeds of a desire, on her part, to repeat the experience. And besides, by holding his tongue his honour remained unimpaired, whereas if he were to talk he would make himself look ridiculous.

And so, showing little sign of his turbulent inner feelings either in his speech or in his facial expression, the King answered her as follows:

'Do you think, my dear, that I am incapable of returning to you a second time after being here once already?'

'Oh no, my lord,' the lady replied. 'But all the same, I beg you not to overdo it.'

'Your advice is sound, and I intend to follow it,' said the King. 'I shall go away again, and bother you no further tonight.'

And so, boiling with anger and indignation because of the trick that had clearly been played upon him, he put on his cloak again and departed, bent upon tracking the culprit quietly down, for the King supposed that he must be a member of the household, in which case, no matter who the fellow was, he would still be within the palace walls.

Accordingly, having equipped himself with a small lantern shedding very little light, he made his way to a dormitory above the palace-stables containing a long row of beds, where nearly all of his servants slept. And since he calculated that the author of the deed to which the lady had referred would not yet have had time to recover a normal pulse and heartbeat after his exertions, the King began at one end of the dormitory and went silently along the row, placing his hand on each man's chest in order to discover whether his heart was still pounding.

Although all the others were sleeping soundly, the one who had been with the Queen was still awake. And when he saw the King approaching, he realized what he was looking for and grew very frightened, with the result that the pounding of his heart, already considerable because of his recent labours, was magnified by his fear. He was convicted that the King would have him instantly put to death if he were to notice the way his heart was racing, and reflected on various possible courses of action. Eventually, however, on observing that the King was unarmed, he decided he would pretend to be asleep and wait for the King to make the first move.

Having examined a large number of the sleepers without finding the man he was looking for, the King came eventually to the groom, and on discovering that his heart was beating strongly, he said to himself: 'This is the one.' Since, however, he had no wish to broadcast his intentions, all he did was to shear away a portion of the hair on one side of the man's head, using a pair of scissors that he had brought along for the purpose. In those days, men wore their hair very long, and the

King left this mark so that he could identify him by it next morning. He then departed from the scene, and returned to his own room.

The groom had witnessed the whole episode, and being of a sharp disposition, he realized all too clearly why he had been marked in this particular fashion. He therefore leapt out of bed without a moment's delay, and having laid his hands on one of several pairs of shears that happened to be kept in the stable for grooming the horses, he silently made the rounds of all the sleeping forms in the dormitory and cut everybody's hair in precisely the same way as his own, just above the ear. Having completed his mission without being detected, he crept back to bed and went to sleep.

When he arose the next morning, the King gave orders for the palace gates to remain closed until his whole household had appeared before him, and they duly assembled in his presence, all of them bare-headed. The King then began to inspect them with the intention of picking out the man whose hair he had shorn, only to discover, to his amazement, that the hair on most of their heads had been cut in exactly similar fashion.

'This fellow I'm looking for may be low-born,' he said to himself, 'but he clearly has all his wits about him.'

Then, realizing that he could not achieve his aim without raising a clamour, and not wishing to bring enormous shame upon himself for the sake of a trifling act of revenge, he decided to deal with the culprit by issuing a stern word of warning and showing him that his deed had not passed undetected.

'Whoever it was who did it,' he said, addressing himself to the whole assembly, 'he'd better not do it again. And now, be off with you.'

Many another man would have wanted to have all of them strung up, tortured, examined and interrogated. But in so doing, he would have brought into the open a thing that people should always try their utmost to conceal. And even if, by displaying his hand, he had secured the fullest possible revenge, he would not have lessened his shame but greatly increased it, as well as besmirching the fame of his lady.

Not unnaturally, the King's little speech caused quite a stir amongst his listeners, and a long time subsequently elapsed before they grew tired of discussing between themselves what it could have meant. But nobody divined its import except the one man for whom it was intended, and he was far too shrewd ever to throw any light on the subject while the King was still alive, nor did he ever risk his life again in performing any deed of a similar nature.

To Catch a Nightingale

Not long ago then, there lived in Romagna a most reputable and virtuous gentleman called Messer Lizio da Valbona, who, on the threshold of old age, had the good fortune to be presented by his wife, Madonna Giacomina, with a baby daughter. When she grew up, she outshone all the other girls in those parts for her charm and beauty, and since she was the only daughter left to her father and mother, they loved and cherished her with all their heart, and guarded her with extraordinary care, for they had high hopes of bestowing her in marriage on the son of some great nobleman.

Now, to the house of Messer Lizio there regularly came a handsome and sprightly youth called Ricciardo de' Manardi da Brettinoro, with whom Messer Lizio spent a good deal of his time; and he and his wife would no more have thought of keeping him under surveillance than if he were their own son. Whenever he set eyes on the girl, Ricciardo was struck by her great beauty, her graceful bearing, her charming ways and impeccable manners, and, seeing that she was of marriageable age, he fell passionately in love with her. He took great pains to conceal his feelings, but the girl divined that he was in love with her, and far from being offended, to Ricciardo's great delight she began to love him with equal fervour. Though frequently seized with the longing to speak to her, he was always too timid to do so until one day, having chosen a suitable moment, he plucked up courage and said to her:

'Caterina, I implore you not to let me die of love for you.'

'Heaven grant,' she promptly replied, 'that you do not allow me to die first for love of you.'

Ricciardo was overjoyed by the girl's answer, and feeling greatly encouraged, he said to her:

'Demand of me anything you please, and I shall do it. But you alone can devise the means of saving us both.'

Whereupon the girl said:

'Ricciardo, as you see, I am watched very closely, and for this reason I cannot think how you are to come to me. But if you are able to suggest anything I might do without bringing shame upon myself, tell me what it is, and I shall do it.'

Ricciardo turned over various schemes in his mind, then suddenly he said:

'My sweet Caterina, the only way I can suggest is for you to come to the balcony overlooking your father's garden, or better still, to sleep there. Although it is very high, if I knew that you were spending the night on the balcony, I would try without fail to climb up and reach you.'

'If you are daring enough to climb to the balcony,' Caterina replied, 'I am quite sure that I can arrange to sleep there.'

Ricciardo assured her that he was, whereupon they snatched a single kiss and went their separate ways.

It was already near the end of May, and on the morning after her conversation with Ricciardo, the girl began complaining to her mother that she had been unable to sleep on the previous night because of the heat.

'What are you talking about, child?' said her mother. 'It wasn't in the least hot.'

To which Caterina said:

'Mother, if you were to add "in my opinion", then perhaps you would be right. But you must remember that young girls feel the heat much more than older women.'

'That is so, my child,' said her mother, 'but what do you expect me to do about it? I can't make it hot or cold for you, just like that. You have to take the weather as it comes, according to the season. Perhaps tonight it will be cooler, and you will sleep better.'

'God grant that you are right,' said Caterina, 'but it is not usual for the nights to grow any cooler as the summer approaches.'

'Then what do you want us to do about it?' inquired the lady.

'If you and father were to consent,' replied Caterina, 'I should like to have a little bed made up for me on the balcony outside his room, overlooking the garden. I should have the nightingale to sing me off to sleep, it would be much cooler there, and I should be altogether better off than I am in your room.'

Whereupon her mother said:

'Cheer up, my child; I shall speak to your father about it, and we shall do whatever he decides.'

The lady reported their conversation to Messer Lizio, who, perhaps because of his age, was inclined to be short-tempered.

'What's all this about being lulled to sleep by the nightingale?' he exclaimed. 'She'll be sleeping to the song of the cicadas if I hear any more of her nonsense.'

Having heard what he had said, on the following night, more to spite her father than because she was feeling hot, Caterina not only stayed awake herself but, by complaining incessantly of the heat, also prevented her mother from sleeping.

So next morning, her mother went straight to Messer Lizio, and said:

'Sir, you cannot be very fond of this daughter of yours. What difference does it make to you whether she sleeps on the balcony or not? She didn't get a moment's rest all night because of the heat. Besides, what do you find so surprising about a young girl taking pleasure in the song of the nightingale? Young people are naturally drawn towards those things that reflect their own natures.'

'Oh, very well,' said Messer Lizio. 'Take whichever bed you please, and set it up for her on the balcony with some curtains round it. Then let her sleep there and hear the nightingale singing to her heart's content.'

On hearing that her father had given his permission, the girl promptly had a bed made up for herself on the balcony; and since it was her intention to sleep there that same night, she waited for Ricciardo to come to the house, and gave him a signal, already agreed between them, by which he understood what was expected of him.

As soon as he had heard his daughter getting into bed, Messer Lizio locked the door leading from his own room to the balcony, and then he too retired for the night.

When there was no longer any sound to be heard, Ricciardo climbed over a wall with the aid of a ladder, then climbed up the side of the house by clinging with great difficulty to a series of stones projecting from the wall. At every moment of the ascent, he was in serious danger of falling, but in the end he reached the balcony unscathed, where he was silently received by the girl with very great rejoicing. After exchanging many kisses, they lay down together and for virtually the entire night they had delight and joy of one another, causing the nightingale to sing at frequent intervals.

Their pleasure was long, the night was brief, and though they were unaware of the fact, it was almost dawn when they eventually fell asleep without a stitch to cover them, exhausted as much by their merry sport as by the nocturnal heat. Caterina had tucked her right arm beneath Ricciardo's neck, whilst with her left hand she was holding that part of his person which in mixed company you ladies are too embarrassed to mention.

Dawn came, but failed to wake them, and they were still asleep in the same posture when Messer Lizio got up out of bed. Remembering that his daughter was sleeping on the balcony, he quietly opened the door, saying:

'I'll just go and see whether Caterina has slept any better with the help of the nightingale.'

Stepping out on to the terrace, he gently raised the curtain surrounding the bed and saw Ricciardo and Caterina, naked and uncovered, lying there asleep in one another's arms, in the posture just described.

Having clearly recognized Ricciardo, he left them there and made his way to his wife's room, where he called to her and said:

'Be quick, woman, get up and come and see, for your daughter was so fascinated by the nightingale that she has succeeded in waylaying it, and is holding it in her hand.'

'What are you talking about?' said the lady.

'You'll see, if you come quickly,' said Messer Lizio.

The lady got dressed in a hurry, and quietly followed in Messer Lizio's footsteps until both of them were beside the bed. The curtain was then raised, and Madonna Giacomina saw for herself exactly how her daughter had taken and seized hold of the nightingale, whose song she had so much yearned to hear.

The lady, who considered that she had been seriously deceived in Ricciardo, was on the point of shouting and screaming abuse at him, but Messer Lizio restrained her, saying:

'Woman, if you value my love, hold your tongue! Now that she has taken him, she shall keep him. Ricciardo is a rich young man, and comes of noble stock. We could do a lot worse than have him as our son-in-law. If he wishes to leave this house unscathed, he will first have to marry our daughter, so that he will have put his nightingale into his own cage and into no other.'

The lady was reassured to see that her husband was not unduly perturbed by what had happened, and on reflecting that her daughter had enjoyed a good night, was well-rested, and had caught the nightingale, she held her peace.

Nor did they have long to wait before Ricciardo woke up, and on seeing that it was broad daylight, he almost died of fright and called to Caterina, saying:

'Alas, my treasure, the day has come and caught me unawares! What is to happen to us?'

At these words, Messer Lizio stepped forward, raised the curtain, and replied:

'What you deserve.'

On seeing Messer Lizio, Ricciardo nearly leapt out of his skin and sat bolt upright in bed, saying:

'My lord, in God's name have mercy on me. I know that I deserve to die, for I have been wicked and disloyal, and hence you must deal with me as you choose. But I beseech you to spare my life, if that is possible. I implore you not to kill me.'

'Ricciardo,' said Messer Lizio, 'this deed was quite unworthy of the love I bore you and the firm trust I placed in you. But what is done cannot be undone, and since it was your youth that carried you into so grievous an error, in order that you may preserve not only your life but also my honour, you must, before you do anything else, take Caterina as your lawful wedded wife. And thus, not only will she have been yours for this night, but she will remain yours for as long as she lives. By this means alone will you secure your freedom and my forgiveness; otherwise you can prepare to meet your Maker.'

Whilst this conversation was taking place, Caterina let go of the nightingale, and having covered herself up, she burst into tears and implored her father to forgive Ricciardo, at the same time beseeching Ricciardo to do as Messer Lizio wished, so that they might long continue to enjoy such nights as this together in perfect safety.

All this pleading was quite superfluous, however, for what with the shame of his transgression and his urge to atone on the one hand, and his desire to escape with his life on the other (to say nothing of his yearning to possess the object of his ardent love), Ricciardo readily consented, without a moment's hesitation, to do what Messer Lizio was asking.

Messer Lizio therefore borrowed one of Madonna Giacomina's rings, and Ricciardo married Caterina there and then without moving from the spot, her parents bearing witness to the event.

This done, Messer Lizio and his wife withdrew, saying:

'Now go back to sleep, for you doubtless stand in greater need of resting than of getting up.'

As soon as Caterina's parents had departed, the two young people fell once more into each other's arms, and since they had only passed half-a-dozen milestones in the course of the night, they added another two to the total before getting up. And for the first day they left it at that.

After they had risen, Ricciardo discussed the matter

in greater detail with Messer Lizio, and a few days later he and Caterina took appropriate steps to renew their marriage vows in the presence of their friends and kinsfolk. Then, amid great rejoicing, he brought her to his house, where the nuptials were celebrated with dignity and splendour. And for many years thereafter he lived with her in peace and happiness, caging nightingales by the score, day and night, to his heart's content.

Oh, to be a Virgin

A long time ago, Babylon was ruled by a sultan called Beminedab, during whose reign it was unusual for anything to happen that was contrary to his wishes. Apart from numerous other children, both male and female, this man possessed a daughter called Alatiel, who, at that period, according to everybody who had set eyes on her, was the most beautiful woman to be found anywhere on earth. Now, the Sultan had recently been attacked by a great horde of Arabs, and inflicted a major defeat on his aggressors, receiving timely assistance from the King of Algarve, who asked the Sultan, as a special favour, to give him Alatiel as his wife. The Sultan agreed, and having seen her aboard a well-armed and well-appointed ship with a retinue of noblemen and noblewomen and a large quantity of elegant and precious accoutrements, he bade her a fond farewell.

Finding the weather favourable, the ship's crew put on full sail, and for several days after leaving Alexandria the voyage was prosperous. But one day, when they had passed Sardinia and were looking forward to journey's end, they ran into a series of sudden squalls, each of which was exceptionally violent, and these gave the ship such a terrible buffeting that passengers and crew were convinced time and again that the end had come.

But they had plenty of spirit, and by exerting all their skill and energy they survived the onslaught of the mountainous seas for two whole days. However, as night approached for the third time since the beginning of the storm, which showed no sign of relenting but on the contrary was increasing in fury, they felt the ship foundering. Though in fact they were not far from the coast of Majorca, they had no idea where they were, because it was a dark night and the sky was covered with thick black clouds, and hence it was impossible to estimate their position either with the ship's instruments or with the naked eye.

It now became a case of every man for himself, and there was nothing for it but to launch a longboat, into which the ship's officers leapt, preferring to put their trust in that rather than in the crippled vessel. But they had no sooner abandoned ship than every man aboard followed their example and leapt into the long-boat, undeterred by the fact that the earlier arrivals were fighting them off with knives in their hands. Thus, in trying to save their lives, they did the exact opposite; for the longboat was not built for holding so many people in weather of this sort and it sank, taking everybody with it.

Meanwhile, the ship itself, though torn open and almost waterlogged, was driven swiftly along by power-ful winds until eventually it ran aground on a beach on the island of Majorca. By this time, the only people still aboard were the lady and her female attendants, and they were all lying there like dead creatures, para-lysed with terror by the raging tempest. The ship's impetus was so great that it thrust its way firmly into the sand before coming to rest a mere stone's throw from the shore, and since the wind was no longer able to move it, there it remained for the rest of the night, to be pounded by the sea.

By the time it was broad daylight, the storm had abated considerably, and the lady, who was feeling practically half-dead, raised her head and began, weak as she was, to call out to her servants one after another. But it was all to no purpose, because they were too far away to hear. On receiving no response and seeing nobody about, she wondered what on earth had happened, and began to be filled with considerable alarm. She staggered to her feet to discover that her maids of honour and the other women were lying about all over the ship, and she attempted to rouse each of them in turn by calling to them at the top of her voice. But few of them showed any signs of life because they had all been laid low by their terror and the heavings of their stomachs, and her own fears were accordingly increased. Nevertheless, since she was all alone and possessed no idea of her whereabouts, she felt in need of someone to talk to, and so she went round prodding the ones who were still alive and forced them to their feet, only to discover that none of them had any idea what had happened to all the men aboard. And when they saw that the ship was aground and full of water, they all started crying as though they would burst.

It was not until mid-afternoon that they were able to make their plight apparent to anybody on the shore or elsewhere in the vicinity who would come to their assistance. Halfway through the afternoon, in fact, a nobleman whose name was Pericone da Visalgo happened to pass that way as he was returning from one of his estates. He was riding along on horseback with several of his men, and when he saw the ship he immediately guessed what had happened. So he ordered one of his servants to try and clamber aboard without further delay and bring him a report on how matters stood. The servant had quite a struggle, but eventually he boarded the ship, where he found the young gentlewoman, frightened out of her senses, hiding with her handful of companions in the forepeak. On seeing him, the women burst into tears and repeatedly pleaded for mercy, but when they perceived that neither he nor they could understand what the other party was saying, they tried to explain their predicament by means of gestures.

Having sized up the situation to the best of his ability, the servant reported his findings to Pericone, who promptly arranged for the women to be brought ashore along with the most valuable of those items on the ship that could be salvaged, and escorted them all to his castle, where he restored the women's spirits by arranging for them to be fed and rested. He could see, from the richness of their apparel, that he had stumbled across some great lady of quality, and he quickly gathered which of them she must be because she was the sole centre of the other women's attention. The lady was pallid and extremely dishevelled-looking as a result of her exhausting experiences at sea, but it seemed to Pericone that she possessed very fine features, and for this reason he resolved there and then that if she had no husband he would marry her, and that, if marriage proved to be out of the question, he would make her his mistress.

Pericone, who was a very powerful, vigorous-looking fellow, caused the lady to be waited upon hand and foot, and when, after a few days, she had fully recovered, he found that she was even more beautiful than he had ever thought possible. He was greatly pained by the fact that they were unable to communicate with each other, and that he could not therefore discover who she was. Nevertheless, being immensely taken with her beauty, he behaved lovingly and agreeably towards her in an endeavour to persuade her to do his pleasure without a struggle. But it was no use: she refused to have anything to do with him; and meanwhile Pericone's ardour continued to increase.

The lady had no idea where she was, but she quickly gathered from their mode of living that the people she was staying with were Christians, and she could see little purpose, even if she had known her whereabouts, in revealing her identity. From the way Pericone was behaving, she knew that sooner or later, whether she liked it or not, she would be compelled to let him have his way with her, but meanwhile she was proudly resolved to turn a blind eye to her sorrowful predicament. To the three surviving members of her female retinue, she gave instructions that they should never disclose their identity to anyone until such time as they were in a position that offered them a clear prospect of freedom. Furthermore, she implored them to preserve their chastity, declaring her own determination to submit to no man's pleasure except her husband's – a sentiment that was greeted with approval by the three women, who said they would do their utmost to follow her instructions.

As the days passed, and Pericone came into closer proximity with the object of his desires, his advances were more firmly rejected, and the flames of his passion raged correspondingly fiercer. Realizing that his flattery was getting him nowhere, he decided to fall back on ingenuity and subterfuge, holding brute strength in reserve as a last resort. He had noticed more than once that the lady liked the taste of wine, which, since it is prohibited by her religion, she was unaccustomed to drinking, and by using this in the service of Venus, he thought it possible that she would yield to him. And so one evening, having feigned indifference concerning the matter for which she had paraded so much distaste, he held a splendid banquet with all the trappings of a great festive occasion, at which the lady was present. The meal was notable for its abundance of good food, and Pericone arranged with the steward who was serving the lady to keep her well supplied with a succession of different wines. The steward carried out his instructions to the letter, and the lady, being caught off her guard and carried away by the agreeable taste of the wines, drank more than was consistent with her decorum. Forgetting all the misfortunes she had experienced, she became positively merry, and when she saw some women dancing in the Majorcan manner, she herself danced Alexandrian fashion.

On seeing this, Pericone felt that he would soon obtain what he wanted, and calling for further large quantities of food and drink, he caused the banquet to continue until the small hours of the morning. Finally, when the guests had departed, he accompanied the lady, alone, into her room. Without the least show of embarrassment, being rather more flushed with wine than tempered by virtue, she then undressed in Pericone's presence as though he were one of her maid-servants, and got into bed. Pericone lost no time in following her example. Having snuffed out all the lights, he quickly scrambled in from the other side and lay down beside her, and taking her into his arms without meeting any resistance on her part, he began making amorous sport with her. She had no conception of the kind of horn that men do their butting with, and when she felt what was happening, it was almost as though she regretted having turned a deaf ear to Pericone's flattery, and could not see why she had waited for an invitation before spending her nights so agreeably. For it was she herself who was now issuing the invitation, and she did so several times over, not in so many words, since she was unable to make herself understood, but by way of her gestures.

Great indeed was their mutual delight. But Fortune, not content with converting her from a king's bride into a baron's mistress, thrust a more terrible friendship upon her.

Pericone had a twenty-five-year-old brother, fair and fresh as a garden rose, whose name was Marato. He had already seen the lady and taken an enormous liking to her, and as far as he could judge from her reactions, she seemed to be very fond of him also. Thus the only thing that appeared to be standing between him and the conquest he desired to make of her was the strict watch maintained by Pericone. He therefore devised a nefarious scheme which he lost no time in pursuing to its dreadful conclusion.

In the port of the town, there happened at that time to be a ship commanded by two young Genoese, with a full cargo for Corinth in the Peloponnese. She was already under canvas, ready to put to sea with the first favourable wind, and Marato made an arrangement with her masters for himself and the lady to be taken aboard the following night. This done, he decided how he would have to proceed, and when it was dark he wandered unobtrusively into his brother's house, to which he had open access, and concealed himself inside.

He had meanwhile enlisted the aid of some trusted companions for his enterprise, and in the dead of night, having let them into the house, he led them to the place where Pericone and the woman were sleeping. Entering the room, they killed Pericone in his sleep and seized the lady, who woke up and started to cry, threatening her with death if she made any noise. Then, taking with them a considerable quantity of Pericone's most precious possessions, they departed without being heard and made their way to the quayside, where Marato boarded the ship with the lady, leaving his companions to go their separate ways.

The ship's crew, taking advantage of a strong and favourable wind, cast off and sailed swiftly away.

The lady was sorely distressed by this second catastrophe, coming as it did so soon after the first. But Marato, with the Heaven-sent assistance of Saint Stiffen-in-the-Hand, began consoling her to such good effect that she soon returned his affection and forgot all about Pericone. She had hardly begun to feel settled, however, before Fortune, not content, it seemed, with her previous handiwork, engineered yet another calamity. As we have almost grown tired of repeating, the woman had the body of an angel and a temperament to match, and the two young masters of the vessel fell so violently in love with her that they could concentrate on nothing else except how best they might make themselves useful and agreeable to her, at the same time taking care not to let Marato see what they were up to.

On discovering that they were both in love with the same woman, they talked the matter over in secret and agreed to make the lady's conquest a mutual affair, as though love were capable of being shared out like merchandise or profits. For some time their plans were thwarted because they found that Marato kept a close watch on her. But one day, when the ship was sailing along like the wind and Marato was standing on the stern facing seaward without the least suspicion of their intentions, they both crept up on him, seized him quickly from behind, and hurled him into the sea. By the time anybody so much as noticed that Marato had fallen overboard, they had already sailed on for over a mile, and the lady, hearing what had happened and seeing no way of going to his rescue, began to fill the whole ship with the sounds of her latest affliction.

The two gallants immediately rushed to her assistance, and with the aid of honeyed words and extravagant promises, few of which she understood, they attempted to pacify her. What she was bemoaning was not so much the loss of Marato as her own sorry plight, and so after she had listened to a stream of fine talk, repeated twice over, she seemed considerably less distraught. The two brothers then got down to a private discussion to decide which of them was to take her off to bed. Each man claimed priority over the other, and having failed to reach any agreement on the matter they began to argue fiercely between themselves. Nor did their quarrel stop with the exchange of verbal abuse. Losing their tempers, they reached for their knives and hurled themselves furiously upon one another, and before the ship's crew could separate the pair, they had both inflicted a number of stab-wounds, from which one man died instantly whilst the other emerged with serious injuries to various parts of his body. The lady was sorely distressed by all this, for she could see that she was now alone on the ship with nobody to turn to for help or advice, and she was greatly afraid lest the relatives and companions of the two men should vent their rage upon her. However, partly because of the injured man's pleas on her behalf, partly because they soon arrived at Corinth, the danger to her person was short-lived. On their arrival, she disembarked with the injured man, and went to live with him at an inn, whence the story of her great beauty spread rapidly through the city, eventually reaching the ears of the

Prince of Morea, who was living in Corinth at that time. He therefore demanded to see her, and on discovering her to be more beautiful than she had been reported, he immediately fell so ardently in love with her that he could think of nothing else.

When he learnt about the circumstances of her arrival in the city, he saw no reason why he should not be able to have her. And indeed, once the wounded man's relatives discovered that the Prince was putting out inquiries, they promptly sent her off to him without asking any questions. The Prince was highly delighted, but so also was the lady, who considered that she had now escaped from a most dangerous situation. On finding that she was endowed with stately manners as well as beauty, the Prince calculated, since he could obtain no other clue to her identity, that she must be a woman of gentle birth, and his love for her was accordingly redoubled. And not only did he keep her in splendid style, but he treated her as though she were his wife rather than his mistress.

On comparing her present circumstances with the awful experiences through which she had passed, the lady considered herself very fortunately placed. Now that she was contented and completely recovered, her beauty flourished to such a degree that the whole of the eastern empire seemed to talk of nothing else. And so it was that the Duke of Athens, a handsome, powerfully proportioned youth who was a friend and relative of the Prince, was smitten with a desire to see her, and under the pretext of paying the Prince one of his customary visits, he came with a splendid and noble retinue to Corinth, where he was received with honour amid great rejoicing.

A few days later, the two men fell to conversing about this woman's beauty, and the Duke asked whether she was so marvellous an object as people claimed.

'Far more so,' replied the Prince. 'But instead of accepting my word for it, I would rather that you judged with your own eyes.'

Thereupon the Prince invited the Duke to follow him, and they made their way to the lady's apartments. Having been warned of their approach, she received them with great civility, her face radiant with happiness. She seated herself between the two men, but the pleasure of conversing with her was denied them because she understood little or nothing of their language. And so each man stared in fascination upon her, in particular the Duke, who could scarcely believe that she was a creature of this earth. Little realizing, as he gazed at her, that he was imbibing the poison of love through the medium of his eyes, and fondly believing that he could satisfy his pleasure merely by looking at her, he was completely bowled over by her beauty and fell violently in love with her.

When he and the Prince had taken their leave of her, and he had an opportunity to indulge in a little quiet reflection, he came to the conclusion that the Prince must be the happiest man on earth, in possessing so beautiful a plaything. Many and varied were the thoughts that passed through his mind until eventually, his blazing passion gaining the upper hand over his sense of honour, he decided that whatever the consequences, he would remove this pleasure-giving object from the Prince and do all in his power to make it serve his own happiness.

Being determined to move swiftly, he thrust aside all regard for reason and fair play, and concentrated solely on cunning. And one day, in the furtherance of his evil designs, he made arrangements with one of the Prince's most trusted servants, Ciuriaci by name, to have all his horses and luggage placed secretly in readiness for a sudden departure. During the night, he and a companion, both fully armed, were silently admitted by the aforesaid Ciuriaci into the Prince's bedroom. It was a very hot night, and although the woman was asleep, the Prince was standing completely naked at a window overlooking the sea, taking advantage of a breeze that was blowing from that quarter. The Duke, having told his companion beforehand what he had to do, stole quietly across the room as far as the window, drove a dagger into the Prince's back with so much force that it passed right through his body, and catching him quickly in his arms he hurled him out of the window.

Now the palace stood very high above sea-level, and the window at which the Prince had been standing overlooked a cluster of houses that had been laid in ruins by the violence of the sea. It was but rarely, if ever, that anybody went there, and consequently, as the Duke had already foreseen, no one's attention was attracted by the body of the Prince as it fell.

On seeing this deed accomplished, the Duke's

companion quickly produced a noose that he had brought along for the purpose, and pretending to embrace Ciuriaci, he threw it round his neck, and drew it tight so that Ciuriaci could not make any noise. He was then joined by the Duke, and they strangled the man before hurling him out to join his master. This done, they satisfied themselves that neither the lady nor anybody else had heard them, and then the Duke picked up a lantern, carried it over to the bed, and silently uncovered the woman, who was sleeping soundly. Having exposed her whole body, he gazed upon her in rapt fascination, and although he had admired her when she was clothed, now that she was naked his admiration was greater beyond all comparison. The flames of his desire burned correspondingly fiercer, and, unperturbed by the crime he had just committed, he lay down at her side, his hands still dripping with blood, and made love to the woman, who was half-asleep and believed him to be the Prince.

Eventually, after spending some time with her, he rose giddily to his feet and summoned a few of his men, whom he commanded to hold the lady in such a way that she could not make any noise. Then he conducted her through the secret door by way of which he had entered, and, having settled her on horseback with a minimum of noise, he set out with all his men in the direction of Athens. Since he was already married, however, it was not in Athens itself that he deposited this unhappiest of women, but at a very beautiful palace of his, not far from the city, overlooking the sea. Here he established her in secluded splendour, and saw that she was provided with everything she needed.

On the following day, the Prince's courtiers had waited until the late afternoon for their master to rise from his bed. But when they still heard no sound, they pushed open his bedroom doors, which were not locked, and found the room deserted. They thereupon assumed that he had gone away somewhere in secret in order to spend a few days in the delightful company of this fair mistress of his, and they gave no further thought to the matter.

It was thus that matters stood, when on the very next day a local idiot, who had strayed into the ruins where the bodies of the Prince and Ciuriaci were lying, dragged Ciuriaci forth by the rope round his neck and started pulling him through the streets. On recognizing who it was, the people were greatly astonished, and talked the idiot into leading them to the place from which he had dragged the body, where, to the enormous grief of the whole city, they also found the body of the Prince. After burying him with full honours, they took steps to discover who was responsible for this unspeakable crime, and on finding that the Duke of Athens had departed secretly and was nowhere to be found, they rightly concluded that he must be the culprit and that he must have carried off the lady as well. So that, having hastily elected their dead ruler's brother as their new prince, they urged him with all the eloquence at their command to take his revenge. And when further evidence came to light, proving that their suspicions were correct, the Prince summoned friends, kinsfolk and servants from various places to come to his support and he quickly assembled a huge and powerful army, with which he set out to make war on the Duke of Athens.

When the Duke received word of the operations, he too mobilized all his armed forces for his defence, and many powerful outsiders came to his assistance, including two who were sent by the Emperor of Constantinople, namely his son, Constant, and his nephew, Manuel. These latter, arriving at the head of large and well-drilled contingents, received a warm welcome from the Duke. But the welcome they received from the Duchess was even warmer, because she was Constant's sister.

With the prospect of war becoming daily more imminent, the Duchess chose a convenient moment to invite the two men to her room, where, talking without stopping amid floods of tears, she told them the whole story, explaining the reasons for the war and exposing the wrong practised upon her by the Duke on account of this woman, of whose existence he imagined her to be ignorant. Bewailing her lot in no uncertain terms, she begged them, for the sake of the Duke's honour and her own happiness, to take whatever measures they could devise for setting matters to rights.

The young men were already fully informed about the whole business, and so without asking too many questions they consoled her to the best of their ability and gave her every ground for optimism. Then, having discovered from the Duchess where the lady was staying, they took their leave of her. Since they had often heard glowing accounts of this woman's marvellous beauty, they were naturally anxious to see her, and they therefore asked the Duke if he would introduce her to them. The Duke agreed to do so, forgetting the fate which had befallen the Prince after granting a similar favour. And the following morning, having ordered a magnificent banquet to be prepared in a beautiful garden on the estate where the lady was living, he took the two men and a handful of other friends to dine with her.

On sitting down in her company, Constant began to stare at her in blank amazement, vowing to himself that he had never seen anything so beautiful, and that no one could possibly reproach the Duke, or anybody else, for resorting to treachery and other dishonest means in order to gain possession of so fair an object. Moreover, his admiration increased with every look he cast in her direction, so that eventually the same thing happened to him as had previously happened to the Duke. And when the time came for him to leave, he was so much in love with her that he dismissed the war completely from his mind and concentrated his thoughts on planning a way of abducting her, at the same time taking good care not to reveal his love to anyone.

But whilst he was struggling with his passion, the time arrived for marching against the Prince, who by now had almost reached the Duke's territories. Accordingly, at a given signal, the Duke set out from Athens with Constant and all the others, and they took up combat positions along certain stretches of the frontier so as to halt the Prince's advance. Constant's thoughts and sentiments continued to focus on the woman, and now that the Duke was no longer near her, he fancied that he had an excellent opportunity for obtaining what he wanted. And so a few days after their arrival at the frontier, he pretended to be seriously ill so that he would have a pretext for returning to Athens. He then handed over all his powers to Manuel, and with the Duke's permission he returned to Athens to stay with his sister. A few days later, having steered the conversation round to the sense of injury under which she was labouring on account of the Duke's mistress, he told her that if she so desired he could be of considerable assistance to her in this affair, in that he could have the woman removed from where she was staying and taken elsewhere.

Thinking that Constant was motivated by brotherly love and not by his love for the woman, the Duchess said that she would be only too pleased, provided it could be carried out in such a way that the Duke never discovered that she had given her consent to the scheme. Constant reassured her completely on this point, and accordingly the Duchess gave him permission to proceed in whatever way he considered best.

The first thing he did was to fit out a fast boat in secret, which one evening, having informed his men on board what they were to do, he sent to a spot near the garden of the place where the lady was living. Then he went there with another group of his men, to be amicably received by her retainers as well as by the lady herself, who, at her visitor's suggestion, accompanied

Constant and his companions into the garden, whilst her servants trailed along behind. As though he wished to impart some message from the Duke, he then led her off alone in the direction of a gate, overlooking the sea, which had already been unlocked by one of his accomplices. At a given signal, the boat nosed her way inshore, and having had the lady seized and bundled quickly aboard, he turned to her servants, saying:

'Unless you want to be killed, don't move or make any sound. It is not my intention to steal the Duke's mistress, but to remove the injury he does to my sister.'

Since nobody dared offer any reply, Constant embarked with his men, settled himself next to the lady, who was crying, and ordered them to cast off and start rowing. And they plied their oars to such good effect that just before dawn on the following day they arrived at Aegina.

Going ashore there in order to rest, Constant amused himself in the company of the lady, who was bitterly bewailing her ill-starred beauty. Then they boarded the ship once again, and a few days later they arrived at Chios, where Constant decided to remain, for he thought he would be safe there from his father's strictures and from the possibility of having to surrender the stolen woman. For several days, the fair lady bemoaned her misfortune. Eventually, however, she responded to Constant's efforts at consoling her, and began, as on previous occasions, to derive pleasure from the fate to which Fortune had consigned her.

And this was how matters stood when Uzbek, who was at that time the King of the Turks and who was constantly at war with the Emperor, happened to pass through Smyrna, where he learned that Constant was leading a dissolute life on Chios with some stolen mistress of his, leaving himself wide open to attack. Arriving by night with a squadron of light warships, Uzbek quietly entered the town with his men, took numerous people captive from their beds before they were aware of their enemies' arrival, and slaughtered those who had woken up in time to seize their arms. The invaders then set the whole town on fire, and having loaded their booty and prisoners on to the ships, they returned to Smyrna.

On reviewing the spoils of the expedition immediately after their return, Uzbek, who was a young man, was delighted to discover the fair lady, whom he recognized as the one who had been taken, along with Constant, as she was lying asleep in her bed. So he promptly married her, and after celebrating the nuptials he happily devoted himself, for the next few months, to the pleasures of the marriage-bed.

Now, during the period immediately preceding these happenings, the Emperor had been negotiating a pact with the King of Cappadocia, Basano, whereby the latter was to descend with his forces on Uzbek from one direction whilst the Emperor attacked him with his own troops from the other. He had not yet been able to bring the negotiations to a successful conclusion, however, because of his unwillingness to concede some of the more outrageous of Basano's demands. But on hearing what had happened to his son, he was so incensed that he immediately agreed to the King of Cappadocia's terms, and urged him to attack Uzbek as soon as he possibly could, meanwhile making his own preparations for marching against him from the opposite direction.

When he heard about this, rather than allow himself to be sandwiched between two mighty rulers, Uzbek assembled his army and marched against the King of Cappadocia, leaving his fair lady at Smyrna under the close supervision of a faithful retainer and friend. Some time later, he confronted and engaged the King of Cappadocia, and in the ensuing battle he was killed, whilst his army was defeated and put to flight. Flushed with victory, Basano began to advance unopposed on Smyrna, and all the people on his route did homage to him as their conqueror.

Meanwhile, the retainer in whose care Uzbek had left his fair lady, Antioco by name, had been so over-whelmed by her beauty that he had betrayed the trust of his friend and master, and although he was getting on in years, he had fallen in love with her. He was familiar with her language, and this pleased her immensely because for several years she had been more or less forced to lead the life of a deaf-mute as she could neither understand what anybody was saying nor make herself understood. With love spurring him on, Antioco began in the first few days to take so many liberties with her that before long they ceased to care about their lord and master who had gone off soldiering to the wars, and not only did they become good friends, they also became lovers. And as they lay between the sheets, they had a very happy time of it together.

But when they heard that Uzbek had been defeated and killed, and that Basano was on his way there, carrying all before him, they decided with one accord not to await his arrival. Taking with them a substantial quantity of Uzbek's most valuable possessions, they fled together in secret and came to Rhodes. But they had not been living there for very long when Antioco became mortally ill. With him at the time there happened to be staying a Cypriot merchant, a bosom friend of his whom he loved dearly, and realizing that his life was drawing to its close, he decided to bequeath his property to him, along with his beloved mistress. And so, shortly before he died, he summoned them both to his bedside, and said:

'I see quite plainly that my strength is failing, which saddens me greatly because life has never been sweeter to me than of late. There is one thing, however, that reconciles me to my fate, for I shall find myself dying – if die I must – in the arms of the two people I love best in the whole world: yours, my dear dear friend, and those of this woman whom I have loved more deeply than I love myself, from the earliest days of our acquaintance. All the same, it worries me to think that when I am gone, she might be left here alone in a strange place, with nobody to turn to for help or advice. And I should be all the more worried if it were not for the knowledge of your own presence, for I believe that you will cherish her, for my sake, as tenderly as you would cherish me. In the event of my death, therefore, I commit her and all my property to your charge, and with all my power I entreat you to handle them both in whatever way you think most likely to console my immortal spirit. And I beseech you, dear sweet lady, not to forget me when I am dead, so that in the next world I can claim to be loved in this world by the fairest woman ever fashioned by Nature. Promise me faithfully that you will carry out these two requests of mine, and I shall undoubtedly die contented.'

As they listened to these words, both the lady and his merchant friend shed many a tear. When he had finished speaking, they soothed him and gave him their word of honour that in the event of his death they would do as he had asked. Very soon afterwards he passed away, and they saw that he was given an honourable funeral.

A few days later, having completed all his business in Rhodes and being desirous of taking ship on a Catalan carrack that was about to sail for Cyprus, the Cypriot merchant inquired of the fair lady what she was proposing to do, telling her that for his part, he was compelled to return to Cyprus. The lady said that if he had no objection, she would gladly accompany him, because she had hoped that out of his affection for Antioco, he would treat and regard her as a sister. The merchant assured her of his willingness to do whatever she asked, and with the object of protecting her from any harm that might befall her before they reached Cyprus, he passed her off as his wife. Having embarked on the ship, therefore, they were assigned to a small cabin on the poop-deck, and in order to maintain appearances, he bedded down with her in the same narrow little bunk. What happened next was something that neither of them had bargained for when leaving Rhodes, because what with the darkness, the enforced idleness, and the warmth of the bed, all of which are powerful stimulants, they were each consumed with an almost equally intense longing, and without sparing a thought for the love and friendship they owed to the dead Antioco, they began to excite each other, with the result that by the time they reached the Cypriot's home-port of Paphos, they had become husband and wife in good earnest. And for some time after their arrival in Paphos, they lived together in the merchant's house.

Now it so happened that there came to Paphos, on some business or other, a gentleman called Antigono, who was old in years and even older in wisdom. He was not a very rich man, because although he had undertaken numerous commissions in the service of the King of Cyprus, Fortune had never been particularly kind to him. One day, as he was walking past the house where the fair lady was living, at a time when the Cypriot merchant was away on a trading mission in Armenia, this Antigono happened to catch sight of the lady at one of the windows. Since she was very beautiful, he began to stare at her, and it occurred to him that he had seen her on some previous occasion, but try as he would he could not remember where.

For a long time now, the fair lady had been a plaything in the hands of Fortune, but the moment was approaching when her trials would be over. When she espied Antigono, she recalled having seen him in

Alexandria, where he once occupied a position of some importance in her father's service. Knowing that her merchant was away, and being suddenly filled with the hope that there might be some possibility of returning once more to her regal status with the help of this man's advice, she sent for him at the earliest opportunity. When he called upon her, she shyly asked whether she was right in thinking him to be Antigono of Famagusta. Antigono said that he was, adding:

'I have an idea, ma'am, that I have seen you before, but I cannot for the life of me remember where. Pray be good enough, therefore, if you have no objection, to remind me who you are.'

On hearing that this was indeed the man she had assumed him to be, the lady burst into tears and threw her arms round his neck, and presently she asked her highly astonished visitor whether he had ever seen her in Alexandria. No sooner had she put the question than Antigono recognized her as the Sultan's daughter Alatiel, whom everybody believed to be drowned at sea, and he prepared to make her the ceremonial bow that was her due. But she would not allow this and asked him instead to come and sit down with her for a while. Complying, Antigono asked her in reverential tones how, when and whence she had come to Cyprus, and told her that the whole Egyptian nation had been convinced, for many years, that she had been drowned at sea.

'I wish to goodness they were right,' said the lady, 'and I think my father would share my opinion if he were ever to discover the sort of life I have led.' And so saying, she started crying prodigiously all over again, whereupon Antigono said to her:

'My lady, it is too soon for you to go upsetting yourself like this. Tell me about your misfortunes, if you like, and about the life you have been living. Possibly we shall find that the point has been reached where we shall be able, with God's help, to devise some happy outcome to your dilemma.'

'Antigono,' the fair lady replied, 'the other day, when I first saw you, it was as if I was seeing my own father. Prompted by the love and tenderness that I have an obligation to bear him, I revealed my presence to you, when I could have remained concealed. Yours is the first familiar face I have encountered for many years, and there are few people I could possibly be so contented to see. To you, therefore, as though you were my father, I shall reveal the story of my appalling misfortunes, which I have never related to anyone before. If, when you have heard what I have to say, you see any possibility of restoring me to my former state, I beseech you to explore it; if not, I must ask you never to tell a living soul that you have either seen me or heard anything about me.'

And so saying, never ceasing to weep, she told him about everything that had happened to her since the day on which she was shipwrecked off Majorca, whereupon Antigono too began to weep with compassion, and after considering the matter at some length, he said:

'My lady, since your identity has remained a secret throughout the course of your misadventures, I shall have no difficulty in restoring you to a higher place than ever in your father's affection, and you will then go to marry the King of Algarve, as originally arranged.'

When she inquired how it was to be managed, he explained to her in detail what she was to do. And to avoid all further delay and any further complications, Antigono returned at once to Famagusta and went to see the King, addressing him thus:

'My lord, if it pleases you, you can at the same time cover yourself with glory and render a most valuable service to one who has grown poor while acting on your behalf. I refer of course to myself.'

The King asked him to explain, and Antigono replied:

'The fair young daughter of the Sultan, who was long reputed to have been drowned at sea, has arrived in Paphos. For many years, she has endured extreme hardship in the struggle to preserve her honour, she has been reduced to comparative poverty, and she wishes to return to her father. If you were to send her back to the Sultan under my escort, it would redound greatly to your credit, and I would be sure of a rich reward. It is unlikely, moreover, that the Sultan will ever forget your charitable deed.'

His regal magnanimity having been stirred, the King readily gave his consent, and he dispatched a guard of honour to accompany the lady to Famagusta, where he and the Queen welcomed her amid scenes of indescribable rejoicing and magnificent pomp and splendour. And when she was asked by the King and Queen to tell them about her adventures, she replied exactly as she had been instructed by Antigono.

A few days later, at her own request, the King sent her back to the Sultan under the guardianship of Antigono, providing her with a distinguished retinue of fine gentlemen and ladies-in-waiting, and needless to say, the Sultan gave her a tremendous welcome, which he extended also to Antigono and the whole of her retinue. After she had rested for a while, the Sultan demanded to know how it came about that she was still alive, where she had been living all this time, and why she had never sent word of what she was doing.

Remembering Antigono's instructions to the tiniest detail, the lady then addressed her father as follows:

'Father, some twenty days after my departure, our ship was disabled by a raging tempest, and ran aground at night on the shores of the western Mediterranean, near a place called Aiguesmortes. I never discovered what happened to all the men who were in the ship. All I can remember is that when the dawn arrived, I truly felt as if I was rising from the dead. The local people had already espied the wreck, and they came running from miles around in order to plunder it. I was put ashore with two of my maidservants, who were instantly snatched by young men and carried off in different directions, and that was the last I saw or heard of them. I myself, after putting up stout resistance, was overpowered by two young men and hauled away by my tresses, weeping bitterly all the time. But just as they were crossing a road in order to drag me into a thick forest, four men happened to pass that way on horseback, and when my captors saw them coming, they instantly let me go and took to their heels.

'On seeing this, the four men, who to judge from their appearance seemed to hold positions of authority, rode swiftly up and asked me a lot of questions, to which I gave as many answers. But it was impossible to make ourselves understood. After talking together for some little while, they took me up on one of their horses and conducted me to a convent of nuns who practised these men's religion. I do not know what it was that they said to the nuns, but at any rate I was kindly received by everybody, and I was always treated with great respect. Whilst there, I joined them in the reverent worship of Saint Stiffen-in-the-Hollows, to whom the women of that country are deeply devoted. But after staying with them for some time, and acquiring a discreet know-ledge of their language, I was asked who I was and where I had come from. Knowing where I was, I feared to tell them the truth lest they should expel me as an enemy of their religion, and so I replied that I was the daughter of a fine nobleman of Cyprus, who was sending me to be married in Crete when we were driven by a storm on to those shores and shipwrecked.

'For fear of meeting a worse fate, I imitated their customs regularly, in various ways. Eventually, I was asked by the oldest of these women, whom the others refer to as the Abbess, whether I wished to return to Cyprus, and I replied that there was nothing I desired more. However, being concerned for my honour, she was unwilling to entrust me to anyone coming to Cyprus until about two months ago, when certain French gentlemen, some of them related to the Abbess, arrived there with their wives. And when she heard that they were going to Jerusalem to visit the Sepulchre, where the man they look upon as God was buried after being killed by the Jews, she placed me under their care and asked them to hand me over to my father on reaching Cyprus.

'It would take too long to describe how greatly I was honoured and how warmly I was welcomed by these noblemen and their wives. Suffice it to say that we all took ship, and that several days later we reached Paphos, where I found myself facing a dilemma, because there was nobody there who knew me and I had no idea what to say to these gentlemen, who were anxious to carry out the venerable lady's instructions and hand me over to my father.

'However, it was the will of Allah, who was possibly feeling sorry for me, that just as we stepped ashore at Paphos Antigono should be standing on the quay-side. I promptly called out to him, and using our own language so that neither the gentlemen nor their wives would follow what I was saying, I told him to welcome me as his daughter. He promptly complied, made a tremendous fuss of me, and strained his modest resources to the limit in ensuring that those noblemen and their ladies were suitably entertained. He after-wards conveyed me to the King of Cyprus, and I could never adequately describe how honourably I was received or how much trouble the King took in returning me to you here in Alexandria. And now, if there is anything else that remains to be said, let it be told by Antigono, to whom I have recounted the story of my adventures over and over again.'

'My lord,' said Antigono, turning to the Sultan, 'her story corresponds in every detail with the account she has given me on many occasions, as well as with the assurances I received from the noblemen in whose company she came to Cyprus. One thing only she has refrained from mentioning because it would not have been appropriate for her to do so, and I shall tell you what it is. Those good people who brought her to Cyprus paid glowing tribute to the honest life she had led while living with the nuns, they were full of praise for her virtue and her excellent character, and when the time came for them to commit her to my charge and bid her a fond farewell, they all, gentlemen and ladies alike, burst into floods of tears. Were I to provide you with a full account of what they said to me on this particular subject, I could go on talking all day and all night without coming to the end of it. I trust, however, that these few remarks will suffice to convince you that, as their words showed and as I have been able to observe for myself, no other living monarch can claim to possess such a beautiful, virtuous and courageous daughter.'

The Sultan was absolutely delighted to hear these tidings, and prayed repeatedly that Allah would grant him an opportunity to make proper restitution to those who had done honour to his daughter, in particular the King of Cyprus who had restored her to him in such splendid style. A few days later, having ordered sumptuous presents to be prepared for Antigono, he gave him leave to return to Cyprus, at the same time dispatching letters and special envoys to convey his heartfelt thanks to the King for the favours he had bestowed upon his daughter.

Then finally, since it was his wish to make an end of what was begun, or in other words that she should become the King of Algarve's wife, he wrote informing him of all that had happened, adding that, if he still desired to marry her, he should send his envoys to fetch her. The King of Algarve was delighted with these tidings, sent a suitably distinguished party to act as her escort, and upon her arrival he gave her a joyous welcome. And so, despite the fact that eight separate men had made love to her on thousands of different occasions, she entered his bed as a virgin and convinced him that it was really so. And for many years afterwards she lived a contented life as his queen. Hence the proverbial saying: 'A kissed mouth docsn't lose its freshness: like the moon it turns up new again.'

Thorns of Desire

Tancredi, Prince of Salerno, was a most benevolent ruler, and kindly of disposition, except for the fact that in his old age he sullied his hands with the blood of passion. In all his life he had but a single child, a daughter, and it would have been better for him if he had never had any at all.

He was as passionately fond of this daughter as any father who has ever lived, and being unable to bring himself to part with her, he refused to marry her off, even when she was several years older than the usual age for taking a husband. Eventually, he gave her to a son of the Duke of Capua, but shortly after her marriage she was left a widow and returned to her father. In physique and facial appearance, she was as beautiful a creature as there ever was; she was youthful and vivacious, and she possessed rather more intelligence than a woman needs. In the house of her doting father she led the life of a great lady, surrounded by comforts of every description. But realizing that her father was so devoted to her that he was in no hurry to make her a second marriage, and feeling that it would be shameless to approach him on the subject, she decided to see whether she could find herself a secret lover who was worthy of her affections.

In her father's court, she encountered many people

of the kind to be found in any princely household, of whom some were nobly bred and others not. Having studied the conduct and manners of several of these, she was attracted to one above all the rest – a young valet of her father's called Guiscardo, who was a man of exceedingly humble birth, but noble in character and bearing. By dint of seeing him often, before very long she fell madly and secretly in love with him, and her admiration of his ways grew steadily more profound. As for the young man himself, not being slow to take a hint, from the moment he perceived her interest in him he lost his heart to her so completely that he could think of virtually nothing else.

And so they were secretly in love with each other. The young woman was longing to be with him, and being unwilling to confide in anyone on the subject of her love, she thought of a novel idea for informing him how they could meet. Having written him a letter, explaining what he was to do in order to be with her on the following day, she inserted it into a length of reed, which later on she handed to Guiscardo, saying as though for the fun of it:

'Turn it into a bellows-pipe for your serving-wench, so that she can use it to kindle the fire this evening.'

Guiscardo took it and went about his business, reflecting that she could hardly have given it to him or spoken as she had without some special motive. As soon as he returned home, he examined the reed, saw that it was split, opened it, and found her letter inside. And when he had read it and taken careful note of what he was to do, he was the happiest man that ever lived, and set about making his preparations for going to see her in the way she had suggested.

Inside the mountain on which the Prince's palace stood, there was a cavern, formed at some remote period of the past, which was partially lit from above through a shaft driven into the hillside. But since the cavern was no longer used, the mouth of the shaft was almost entirely covered over by weeds and brambles. There was a secret staircase leading to the cavern from a room occupied by the lady, on the ground-floor of the palace, but the way was barred by a massive door. So many years had passed since the staircase had last been used, that hardly anybody remembered it was still there; but Love, to whose eyes nothing remains concealed, had reminded the enamoured lady of its existence.

For several days, she had been struggling to open this door by herself, using certain implements of her own as picklocks so that no one should perceive what was afoot. Having finally got it open, she had descended alone into the cavern, seen the shaft, and written to Guiscardo, giving him a rough idea of the distance between the top of the shaft and the floor of the cavern, and telling him to try and use the shaft as his means of access. With this object in view, Guiscardo promptly got hold of a suitable length of rope, tied various knots and loops in it to allow him to climb up and down, and the following night, without breathing a word to anyone, he made his way to the shaft, wearing a suit of leather to protect himself from the brambles. Firmly tying one end of the rope to a stout bush that had taken root at the mouth of the opening, he lowered himself into the cavern and waited for the lady to come.

In the course of the following day, the princess dismissed her ladies-in-waiting on the pretext of wanting to sleep, and having locked herself in her chamber, she opened the door and descended into the cavern, where she found Guiscardo waiting. After giving each other a rapturous greeting, they made their way into her chamber, where they spent a goodly portion of the day in transports of bliss. Before parting, they agreed on the wisest way of pursuing their lovemaking in future so that it should remain a secret, and then Guiscardo returned to the cavern, whilst the princess, having bolted the door behind him, came forth to rejoin her ladies-in-waiting.

During the night, Guiscardo climbed back up the rope, made his way out through the aperture by which he had entered, and returned home. And now that he was conversant with the route, he began to make regular use of it.

But their pleasure, being so immense and so continuous, attracted the envy of Fortune, who brought about a calamity, turning the joy of the two lovers into tears and sorrow.

From time to time, Prince Tancredi was in the habit of going alone to visit his daughter, with whom he would stay and converse for a while in her chamber and then go away. And one day, after breakfast, he came down to see her, entering her room without anyone hearing or noticing, only to discover that the princess (whose name was Ghismonda) had gone into her garden with all her ladies-in-waiting. Not wishing to disturb her whilst she was enjoying her walk in the garden, he sat down to wait for her on a low stool at a corner of her bed. The windows of the room were closed, and the bed-curtains had been drawn aside, and Tancredi rested his head against the side of the bed, drew the curtain round his body as though to conceal himself there on purpose, and fell asleep.

Whilst he was asleep, Ghismonda, who unfortunately had made an appointment with Guiscardo for that very day, left her attendants in the garden and stole quietly into the room, locking herself in without perceiving that anyone was there. Having opened the door for Guiscardo, who was waiting for her, they then went to bed in the usual way; but whilst they were playing and cavorting together, Tancredi chanced to wake up, and heard and saw what Guiscardo and his daughter were doing. The sight filled him with dismay, and at first he wanted to cry out to them, but then he decided to hold his peace and, if possible, remain hidden, so that he could carry out, with greater prudence and less detriment to his honour, the plan of action that had already taken shape in his mind.

The two lovers remained together for a considerable time, as was their custom, without noticing Tancredi; and when they felt it was time for them to part, they got up from the bed and Guiscardo returned to the cavern. Ghismonda too left the room, and Tancredi, though he was getting on in years, clambered through a window and lowered himself into the garden without being seen, returning thence in deep distress to his own apartment.

On Tancredi's orders, Guiscardo was taken prisoner by two guards soon after dark that very night, just as he was emerging, hindered by the suit of leather he was wearing, from the hole in the ground. He was then conducted in secret to Tancredi, who almost burst into tears on seeing him, and said:

'Guiscardo, my benevolence towards you deserved a better reward than the shameful deed I saw you committing today, with my own eyes, against that which belongs to me.'

By way of reply, all that Guiscardo said was:

'Neither you nor I can resist the power of Love.'

Tancredi then ordered him to be placed under secret guard in one of the inner rooms, and this was done.

Ghismonda knew nothing of this, and after breakfast on the next day, Tancredi, who had been thinking all manner of strange and terrible thoughts, paid his usual call upon his daughter in her chamber. And having locked the door behind him, his eyes filled with tears, and he said to her:

'Never having doubted your virtue and honesty, Ghismonda, it would never have occurred to me, what-ever people might have said, that you would ever so much as think of yielding to a man who was not your husband. But now I have actually seen you doing it with my own eyes, and the memory of it will always torment me during what little remains of my old age.

'Moreover, since you felt bound to bring so much dishonour upon yourself, in God's name you might at least have chosen someone whose rank was suited to your own. But of all the people who frequent my court, you have to choose Guiscardo, a youth of exceedingly base condition, whom we took into our court and raised from early childhood mainly out of charity. Your conduct has faced me with an appalling dilemma, inasmuch as I have no idea how I am to deal with you. I have already come to a decision about Guiscardo, who is under lock and key, having been arrested last night on my orders as he was emerging from the cavern; but God knows what I am to do with you. I am drawn in one direction by the love I have always borne you, deeper by far than that of any other father for a daughter; but on the other hand I seethe with all the indignation that the folly of your actions demands. My love prompts me to forgive you; my indignation demands that I should punish you without mercy, though it would be against my nature to do so. But before I reach any decision, I should like to hear what you have to say for yourself on the subject.' And so saying, he lowered his gaze and began to wail as though he were a child who had been soundly beaten.

Realizing, from what her father had said, that not only had her secret been discovered but Guiscardo was captured, Ghismonda was utterly overcome with sorrow, and needed all the self-control she possessed to prevent herself from screaming and sobbing as most other women would have done. But her proudness of heart more than made up for her shattered spirits, and by a miraculous effort of will, she remained impassive, and rather than make excuses for herself, she resolved to live no longer, being convinced that her Guiscardo was already dead.

She therefore allowed no trace of contrition or womanly distress to cloud her features, but addressed her father in a firm, unworried voice, staring him straight in the face without a single tear in her eyes.

'Tancredi,' she said, 'I am resolved neither to contradict you nor to implore your forgiveness, because denial would be pointless and I want none of your clemency. Nor do I have the slightest intention of appealing either to your better nature or to your affection. On the contrary, I propose to tell you the whole truth, setting forth convincing arguments in defence of my good name, and afterwards I shall act unflinchingly in accordance with the promptings of my noble heart. It is true that I loved Guiscardo, and that I love him still. I shall continue to love him until I die, which I expect to do very soon. And if people love each other beyond the grave, I shall never cease to love him. I was prompted to act as I did, not so much by my womanly frailty as by your lack of concern to marry me, together with his own outstanding worth. You are made of flesh and blood, Tancredi, and it should have been obvious to you that the daughter you fathered was also made of flesh and blood, and not of stone or iron. Although you are now an old man, you should have remembered, indeed you should still remember, the nature and power of the laws of youth. And although much of your own youth was spent in pursuit of military glory, you should none the less have realized how the old and the young are alike affected by living in comfort and idleness.

'As I have said, since you were the person who fathered me, I am made of flesh and blood like yourself. Moreover, I am still a young woman. And for both of these reasons, I am full of amorous longings, intensified beyond belief by my marriage, which enabled me to discover the marvellous joy that comes from their fulfilment. As I was incapable of resisting these forces, I made up my mind, being a woman in the prime of life, to follow the path along which they were leading, and I fell in love. But though I was prepared to commit a natural sin, I was determined to spare no effort to ensure that neither your good name nor mine should suffer any harm. To this end, I was assisted by compassionate Love and benign Fortune, who taught me the means whereby I could secretly achieve the fulfilment of my desires. No matter who told you about my secret, no matter how you came to discover it, I do not deny that the thing has happened.

'I did not take a lover at random, as many women do, but deliberately chose Guiscardo in preference to any other, only conceding my love to him after careful reflection; and through the patience and good judgement of us both, I have long been enjoying the gratification of my desires. It seems, however, that you prefer to accept a common fallacy rather than the truth, for you reproach me more bitterly, not for committing the crime of loving a man, but for consorting with a person of lowly rank, thus implying that if I had selected a nobleman for the purpose, you would not have had anything to worry about. You clearly fail to realize that in this respect, your strictures should be aimed, not at me, but at Fortune, who frequently raises the unworthy to positions of eminence and leaves the worthiest in low estate.

'But leaving this aside, consider for a moment the principles of things, and you will see that we are all of one flesh and that our souls were created by a single Maker, who gave the same capacities and powers and faculties to each. We were all born equal, and still are, but merit first set us apart, and those who had more of it, and used it the most, acquired the name of nobles to distinguish them from the rest. Since then, this law has been obscured by a contrary practice, but nature and good manners ensure that its force still remains unimpaired; hence any man whose conduct is virtuous proclaims himself a noble, and those who call him by any other name are in error.

'Consider each of your nobles in turn, compare their lives, their customs and their manners with those of Guiscardo, and if you judge the matter impartially, you will conclude that he alone is a patrician whilst all these nobles of yours are plebeians. Besides, it was not through hearsay that Guiscardo's merit and virtues came to my notice, but through your good opinion of him, together with the evidence of my own eyes. For was it not you yourself who sang his praises more loudly than any, claiming for him all the qualities by which one measures a man's excellence? Nor were you mistaken by any means, for unless my eyes have played me false, I have seen him practise the very virtues for which you commended him, in a manner more wonderful than your words could express. So that if I was deceived in my estimate of Guiscardo, it was you alone who deceived me.

'If, then, you maintain that I gave myself to a man of base condition, you are wrong. If, on the other hand, you were to describe him as poor, then perhaps you would be right, and you should hang your head in shame for the paltry rewards you bestowed on so excellent a servant. But in any case, a man's nobility is not affected by poverty, as it is by riches. Many kings, many great princes, were once poor; many a ploughman or shepherd, not only in the past but in the present, was once exceedingly wealthy.

'As for the last of your dilemmas, concerning how you are to deal with me, you can dismiss it from your thoughts entirely. If you are intent, in your extreme old age, upon behaving as you never behaved in your youth, and resorting to cruelty, then let your cruelty be aimed at me, for it was I who caused this so-called sin to be committed. I am resolved not to plead for clemency, and I swear that unless you do the same to me as you have already done, or intend to do, to Guiscardo, these hands of mine will do it for you.

'Now get you hence to shed your tears among the women, and if you think we have earned your cruelty, see that you slaughter us both at one and the same time.'

Although Tancredi knew that his daughter had a will of iron, he doubted her resolve to translate her words into action. So he went away and decided that whilst he would dismiss all thought of venting his rage on Ghismonda, he would cool her ardent passion by taking revenge on her lover. He therefore ordered the two men who were guarding Guiscardo to strangle him noiselessly that same night, after which they were to take out his heart and bring it to him; and they carried out his orders to the letter.

Early next day, the Prince called for a fine, big chalice made of gold, and having placed Guiscardo's heart inside it, he ordered one of his most trusted servants to take it to his daughter, bidding him utter these words as he handed it over: 'Your father sends you this to comfort you in the loss of your dearest possession, just as you have comforted him in the loss of his.'

After her father had left, Ghismonda, unflinching in her harsh resolve, had called for poisonous herbs and roots, which she then distilled and converted into a potion, so that, if things turned out as she feared, she would have it ready to hand. And when the servant came to her with her father's gift and recited the message, she accepted it with great composure and removed the lid, no sooner seeing the heart and hearing the servant's words than she knew for certain that this was the heart of Guiscardo.

So she looked up at the servant, and said to him:

'Nothing less splendid than a golden sepulchre would have suited so noble a heart; in this respect, my father has acted wisely.'

Having spoken these words, she raised it to her lips and kissed it, then continued:

'Throughout my life, which is now approaching its end, I have had constant reminders of my father's devoted love, but never so patent a token as this. And in thanking him for the last time, I bid you tell him how grateful I was for so priceless a gift.'

Then she turned to the chalice, which she was holding firmly in her two hands, and gazing down upon Guiscardo's heart, she said:

'Ah! dear, sweet vessel of all my joys, cursed be the cruelty of him who has compelled me to see you with the eyes of my body, when it was enough that I should keep you constantly in the eyes of my mind! Your life has run the brief course allotted to it by Fortune, you have reached the end to which all men hasten, and in leaving behind the trials and tribulations of our mortal life, you have received at the hands of your enemy a burial worthy of your excellence. Your funeral rites lacked nothing but the tears of the woman you loved so dearly; but so that you should not be without them, God impelled my pitiless father to send you to me, and I shall cry for you even though I had resolved to die with tearless eyes and features unclouded by fear. And the instant my tears are finished I shall see that my soul is united with that other soul which you kept in your loving care. How could I wish for a better or surer companion as I set forth towards the unknown? I feel certain that his soul still lingers here within you, waiting for mine and surveying the scenes of our mutual happiness, and that our love for one another is as deep and enduring as ever.'

She said no more, but leaned over the chalice, suppressing all sound of womanly grief, and began to cry in a fashion wondrous to behold, her tears gushing forth like water from a fountain; and she implanted countless kisses upon the lifeless heart.

Her ladies-in-waiting, by whom she was surrounded, were at a loss to know what heart this was, nor were they able to make any sense of her words, but they too began to cry in unison, being filled with compassion for their mistress. They pleaded with her to explain why she was weeping, but to no avail; and for all their strenuous efforts, they were unable to console her.

But when she had cried as much as she deemed sufficient, she raised her head from the chalice, and after drying her eyes, she said:

'Oh, heart that I love so dearly, now that I have fully discharged my duties towards you, all that remains to be done is to bring my soul and unite it with yours.'

Having pronounced these words, she called for the phial containing the potion she had prepared on the previous day, and, pouring it into the chalice, where the heart lay bathed in her own abundant tears, she raised the mixture to her lips without any show of fear and drank it. After which, still holding on to the chalice, she climbed on to her bed, arranged herself as decorously as she could, and placing the heart of her dead lover close to her own, she silently waited for death.

Her ladies-in-waiting had no idea what potion it was that she had drunk, but her speech and actions were so strange that they had sent to inform Tancredi of all that was happening, and he, fearing the worst, had hurried down at once to his daughter's chamber, arriving there just as she had settled herself upon the bed. On seeing the state she was in, he tried to console her with honeyed words, and burst into floods of tears, but the time for pity was past, and Ghismonda said to him:

'Save those tears of yours for a less coveted fate than this of mine, Tancredi, and shed them not for me, for I do not want them. Who ever heard of anyone, other than yourself, who wept on achieving his wishes? But if you still retain some tiny spark of your former love for me, grant me one final gift, and since it displeased you that I should live quietly with Guiscardo in secret, see that my body is publicly laid to rest beside his in whatever spot you chose to cast his remains.'

The vehemence of his sobbing prevented the Prince from offering any reply, and the young woman, sensing that she was about to breathe her last, clasped the dead heart tightly to her bosom, saying:

'God be with you all, for I now take my leave of you.'

Then her vision grew blurred, she lost the use of her senses, and she left this life of sorrow behind her.

Thus the love of Guiscardo and Ghismonda came to its sad conclusion, as you have now heard. And as for Tancredi, after shedding countless tears and making tardy repentance for his cruelty, he saw that they were honourably interred together in a single grave, amid the general mourning of all the people of Salerno.

Head in the Herbs

In Messina, there once lived three brothers, all of them merchants who had been left very rich after the death of their father, whose native town was San Gimignano. They had a sister called Lisabetta, but for some reason or other they had failed to bestow her in marriage, despite the fact that she was uncommonly gracious and beautiful.

In one of their trading establishments, the three brothers employed a young Pisan named Lorenzo, who planned and directed all their operations, and who, being rather dashing and handsomely proportioned, had often attracted the gaze of Lisabetta. Having noticed more than once that she had grown exceedingly fond of him, Lorenzo abandoned all his other amours and began in like fashion to set his own heart on winning Lisabetta. And since they were equally in love with each other, before very long they gratified their dearest wishes, taking care not to be discovered.

In this way, their love continued to prosper, much to their common enjoyment and pleasure. They did everything they could to keep the affair a secret, but one night, as Lisabetta was making her way to Lorenzo's sleeping-quarters, she was observed, without knowing it, by her eldest brother. The discovery greatly distressed him, but being a young man of some intelligence, and not wishing to do anything that would bring discredit upon his family, he neither spoke nor made a move, but spent the whole of the night applying his mind to various sides of the matter.

Next morning he described to his brothers what he had seen of Lisabetta and Lorenzo the night before, and the three of them talked the thing over at considerable length. Being determined that the affair should leave no stain upon the reputation either of themselves or of their sister, he decided that they must pass it over in silence and pretend to have neither seen nor heard anything until such time as it was safe and convenient for them to rid themselves of this ignominy before it got out of hand.

Abiding by this decision, the three brothers jested and chatted with Lorenzo in their usual manner, until one day they pretended they were all going off on a pleasure-trip to the country, and took Lorenzo with them. They bided their time, and on reaching a very remote and lonely spot, they took Lorenzo off his guard, murdered him, and buried his corpse. No one had witnessed the deed, and on their return to Messina they put it about that they had sent Lorenzo away on a trading assignment, being all the more readily believed as they had done this so often before.

Lorenzo's continued absence weighed heavily upon Lisabetta, who kept asking her brothers, in anxious tones, what had become of him, and eventually her questioning became so persistent that one of her brothers rounded on her, and said:

'What is the meaning of this? What business do you

have with Lorenzo, that you should be asking so many questions about him? If you go on pestering us, we shall give you the answer you deserve.'

From then on, the young woman, who was sad and miserable and full of strange forebodings, refrained from asking questions. But at night she would repeatedly utter his name in a heart-rending voice and beseech him to come to her, and from time to time she would burst into tears because of his failure to return. Nothing would restore her spirits, and meanwhile she simply went on waiting.

One night, however, after crying so much over Lorenzo's absence that she eventually cried herself off to sleep, he appeared to her in a dream, pallid-looking and all dishevelled, his clothes tattered and decaying, and it seemed to her that he said:

'Ah, Lisabetta, you do nothing but call to me and bemoan my long absence, and you cruelly reprove me with your tears. Hence I must tell you that I can never return, because on the day that you saw me for the last time, I was murdered by your brothers.'

He then described the place where they had buried him, told her not to call to him or wait for him any longer, and disappeared.

Having woken up, believing that what she had seen was true, the young woman wept bitterly. And when she arose next morning, she resolved to go to the place and seek confirmation of what she had seen in her sleep. She dared not mention the apparition to her brothers, but obtained their permission to make a brief trip to the country for pleasure, taking with her a maidservant who had once acted as her go-between and was privy to all her affairs. She immediately set out, and on reaching the spot, swept aside some dead leaves and started to excavate a section of the ground that appeared to have been disturbed. Nor did she have to dig very deep before she uncovered her poor lover's body, which, showing no sign as yet of decomposition or decay, proved all too clearly that her vision had been true. She was the saddest woman alive, but knowing that this was no time for weeping, and seeing that it was impossible for her to take away his whole body (as she would dearly have wished), she laid it to rest in a more appropriate spot, then severed the head from the shoulders as best she could and enveloped it in a towel. This she handed into her maidservant's keeping whilst she covered over the remainder of the corpse with soil, and then they returned home, having completed the whole of their task unobserved.

Taking the head to her room, she locked herself in and cried bitterly, weeping so profusely that she saturated it with her tears, at the same time implanting a thousand kisses upon it. Then she wrapped the head in a piece of rich cloth, and laid it in a large and elegant pot, of the sort in which basil or marjoram is grown. She next covered it with soil, in which she planted several sprigs of the finest Salernitan basil, and never watered them except with essence of roses or orange-blossom, or with her own teardrops. She took to sitting permanently beside this pot and gazing lovingly at it, concentrating the whole of her desire upon it because it was where her beloved Lorenzo lay concealed. And after gazing raptly for a long while upon it, she would bend over it and begin to cry, and her weeping never ceased until the whole of the basil was wet with her tears.

Because of the long and unceasing care that was lavished upon it, and also because the soil was enriched by the decomposing head inside the pot, the basil grew very thick and exceedingly fragrant. The young woman constantly followed this same routine, and from time to time she attracted the attention of her neighbours. And as they had heard her brothers expressing their concern at the decline in her good looks and the way in which her eyes appeared to have sunk into their sockets, they told them what they had seen, adding:

'We have noticed that she follows the same routine every day.'

The brothers discovered for themselves that this was so, and having reproached her once or twice without the slightest effect, they caused the pot to be secretly removed from her room. When she found that it was missing, she kept asking for it over and over again, and because they would not restore it to her she sobbed and cried without a pause until eventually she fell seriously ill. And from her bed of sickness she would call for nothing else except her pot of basil.

The young men were astonished by the persistence of her entreaties, and decided to examine its contents. Having shaken out the soil, they saw the cloth and found the decomposing head inside it, still sufficiently intact for them to recognize it as Lorenzo's from the curls of his hair. This discovery greatly amazed them, and they were afraid lest people should come to know what had happened. So they buried the head, and without breathing a word to anyone, having wound up their affairs in Messina, they left the city and went to live in Naples.

The girl went on weeping and demanding her pot of basil, until eventually she cried herself to death, thus bringing her ill-fated love to an end. But after due process of time, many people came to know of the affair, and one of them composed the song which can still be heard to this day:

> Whoever it was,
> Whoever the villain
> That stole my pot of herbs, etc.

Poor Man's Poison

As we have already had occasion to remark, whilst Love readily sets up house in the mansions of the aristocracy, this is no reason for concluding that he declines to govern the dwellings of the poor. On the contrary, he sometimes chooses such places for a display of strength no less awe-inspiring than that used by a mighty overlord to intimidate the richest of his subjects. Though the proof will not be conclusive, this assertion will in large measure be confirmed by my story, which offers me the pleasing prospect of returning to your fair city, whence, in the course of the present day, ranging widely over diverse subjects and directing our steps to various parts of the world, we have strayed so far afield.

Not so very long ago, then, there lived in Florence a young woman called Simona, a poor man's daughter, who, due allowance being made for her social condition, was exceedingly gracious and beautiful. Although she was obliged to earn every morsel that passed her lips by working with her hands, and obtained her livelihood by spinning wool, she was not so faint-hearted as to close her mind to Love, which for some time had been showing every sign of wishing to enter her thoughts via the agreeable words and deeds of a youth no more

highly placed than herself, who was employed by a
wool-merchant to go round and distribute wool for
spinning. Having thus admitted Love to her thoughts
in the pleasing shape of this young man, whose name
was Pasquino, she was filled with powerful yearnings
but was too timid to do anything about them. And as
she sat at her spinning and recalled who had given her
the wool, she heaved a thousand sighs more torrid than
fire for every yard of woollen thread that she wound
round her spindle. For his part, Pasquino developed a
special interest in seeing that his master's wool was
properly spun, and, acting as though the finished cloth
was to consist solely of the wool that Simona was
spinning, and no other, he encouraged her far more
assiduously than any of the other girls. The young
woman responded well to Pasquino's encouragement.
She cast aside a good deal of her accustomed modesty
and reserve, whilst he acquired greater daring than
was usual for him, so that eventually, to their mutual
pleasure and delight, their physical union was achieved.
This sport they found so much to their liking that
neither waited to be asked to play it by the other, but
it was rather a question whenever they met of who was
going to be first to suggest it.

With their pleasure thus continuing from one day to
the next and waxing more impassioned in the process,
Pasquino chanced to say to Simona that he would
dearly like her to contrive some way of meeting him in
a certain garden, whither he was anxious for her to
come so that they could feel more relaxed together and
less apprehensive of discovery.

Simona agreed to do it, and one Sunday, immediately after lunch, having given her father to understand that she was going to the pardoning at San Gallo, she made her way with a companion of hers called Lagina to the garden Pasquino had mentioned. When she got there, she found him with a friend of his whose name was Puccino, but who was better known as Stramba, or Dotty Joe. Stramba hit it off with Lagina from the very beginning, and so Simona and Pasquino left them together in one part of the garden and withdrew to another to pursue their own pleasures.

In that part of the garden to which Simona and Pasquino had retired, there was a splendid and very large clump of sage, at the foot of which they settled down to amuse themselves at their leisure. Some time later, having made frequent mention of a picnic they were intending to take, there in the garden, after they had rested from their exertions, Pasquino turned to the huge clump of sage and detached one of its leaves, with which he began to rub his teeth and gums, claiming that sage prevented food from sticking to the teeth after a meal.

After rubbing them thus for a while, he returned to the subject of the picnic about which he had been talking earlier. But before he had got very far, a radical change came over his features, and very soon afterwards he lost all power of sight and speech. A few minutes later he was dead, and Simona, having witnessed the whole episode, started crying and shrieking and calling out to Stramba and Lagina. They promptly rushed over to the spot, and when Stramba saw that not only was

Pasquino dead, but his face and body were already covered with swellings and dark blotches, he exclaimed:

'Ah! you foul bitch, you've poisoned him!'

He made such a din that he was heard by several of the people living in the neighbourhood of the garden, and they rushed to see what it was all about. On finding this fellow lying there, dead and swollen, and hearing Stramba taking it out on Simona and accusing her of having tricked Pasquino into taking poison, whilst the girl herself, grief-stricken because of the sudden death of her lover, was so obviously at a loss for an explanation, they all concluded that Stramba's version of what had happened must be correct.

She was therefore seized and taken to the palace of the *podestà*, shedding copious tears all the way. Stramba had by this time been joined by two other friends of Pasquino, who were known as Atticciato and Malagevole, or in other words, Potbelly and Killjoy, and the three of them stirred up so much fuss that a judge was persuaded to interrogate her forthwith about the circumstances of Pasquino's death. But being unable to conceive how Simona could have practised any deceit, or how she could possibly be guilty, he insisted that she should accompany him to the site of the occurrence, so that, by getting her to show him the manner of it and seeing the dead body for himself, he could form a clearer impression of the matter than he had been able to obtain from her words alone.

Without creating any disturbance, he therefore had her conveyed to the spot where Pasquino's body lay, still swollen up like a barrel, and shortly afterwards he went there himself. Gazing at the body in astonishment, he asked her to show him precisely how it had happened, whereupon Simona walked over to the clump of sage, and, having told the judge what they had been doing together so as to place him fully in possession of the facts, she did as Pasquino had done, and rubbed one of the sage-leaves against her teeth.

Simona's actions were greeted with hoots of derision by Stramba, Atticciato, and Pasquino's other friends and acquaintances, who told the judge that they were pointless and frivolous, and denounced her wickedness with greater vehemence, at the same time demanding that she be burnt at the stake, since no lesser punishment would be appropriate for so terrible a crime. The poor creature was petrified, not only on account of her sorrow at losing her lover, but also because of her fear of suffering the punishment demanded by Stramba. But suddenly, as the result of having rubbed the sage-leaf against her teeth, she met the very same fate as the one that had befallen Pasquino, to the no small amazement of all those present.

Oh, happy souls, who within the space of a single day were granted release from your passionate love and your mortal existence! And happier still, if your destination was shared! And happy beyond description, if love is possible after death, and you love one another in the after-life as deeply as you did on earth! But happiest of all, so far as we, who have survived her, are able to judge, is the soul of Simona herself, since Fortune preserved her innocence against the testimony of Stramba and Atticciato and Malagevole – who were certainly worth no more than a trio of carders, and possibly even less – and, by causing her to die in the same way as her lover, found a more seemly way of ending her misery. For not only was she able to clear herself from their slanderous allegations, but she went to join the soul of her beloved Pasquino.

The judge, along with all the others present, was hardly able to believe his eyes, and remained rooted to the spot for some little time, not knowing what to say. But eventually, he recovered his wits, and said:

'The sage is evidently poisonous, which is rather unusual, to say the least. Before it should claim any further victims, let it be hacked down to its roots and set on fire.'

In the judge's presence, the man in charge of the garden proceeded to carry out these instructions, but he had no sooner felled the giant clump than the reason for the deaths of the two poor lovers became apparent.

Crouching beneath the clump of sage, there was an incredibly large toad, by whose venomous breath they realized that the bush must have been poisoned. Nobody dared to approach it, and so they surrounded it with a huge pyre, and cremated it alive together with the sage-bush. So ended the investigation of His Worship into the death of poor Pasquino, whose swollen body, together with that of his beloved Simona, was buried by Stramba and Atticciato and Guccio Imbratta and Malagevole in the Church of Saint Paul, which happened to be the parish to which the two dead lovers belonged.

The Loving Corpse

Now, there is nothing in the whole of Nature that is less susceptible to advice or interference than Love, whose qualities are such that it is far more likely to burn itself out of its own free will than be quenched by deliberate pressure. And so it occurs to me that I should tell you a story about a lady who, in the belief that she could remove, from an enamoured heart, a love which had possibly been planted there by the stars, sought to be wiser than she actually was, and by flaunting her cleverness in a matter that was beyond her competence, succeeded at one and the same time in driving both Love and life from the body of her son.

According to the tales of our elders, there once lived in our city a very powerful and wealthy merchant whose name was Leonardo Sighieri, who had a son from his wife called Girolamo, and who, after the child was born, carefully put all his affairs in order and departed this life. The boy's interests were skilfully and scrupulously managed by his guardians, acting in conjunction with his mother. He grew up with the children of other families in the neighbourhood, and became very attached to a little girl of his own age, who was the daughter of a tailor. As they grew older, their friendship ripened into a love so great and passionate that

Girolamo could not bear to let her out of his sight, and her own regard for him was certainly no less extreme. On perceiving this, the boy's mother took him to task several times, and even punished him for it. But on finding that he could not be deterred, she took the matter up with the boy's guardians, being convinced that because of her son's great wealth she could, as it were, turn a plum into an orange.

'This boy of ours,' she told them, 'who has only just reached the age of fourteen, is so enamoured of a local tailor's daughter, Salvestra by name, that if we do not separate them we shall perhaps wake up one morning to find that he has married her without telling anyone about it, and I shall never be happy again. If on the other hand he sees her marrying another, he will pine away. And so it would seem to me that in order to nip the affair in the bud, you ought to pack him off to some distant part of the world in the service of the firm. For if he is prevented from seeing the girl over a long period, she will vanish from his thoughts and we shall then be able to marry him to some young lady of gentle breeding.'

The guardians agreed with the lady's point of view and assured her that they would do all in their power to carry out her proposal. And having sent for the boy at the firm's premises, one of them began talking to him in tones of great affection, saying:

'My boy, you are quite a big fellow now, and it would be a good thing for you to start attending to your own affairs. We would therefore be very happy if you were to go and stay for a while in Paris, where you will not only see how a sizeable part of your business is managed, but you will also, by mixing with all those lords and barons and nobles who abound in that part of the world, become a much better man, and acquire greater experience and refinement, than by remaining here. And then you can return to Florence.'

Having listened carefully, the lad gave them a short answer, saying that he would have none of it, since he considered he had as much right as anyone else to remain in Florence. His worthy mentors made several further attempts to persuade him, but being unable to extract any different answer, they reported back to the mother. She was livid with anger, and gave him a fierce scolding, not because he did not want to go to Paris but on account of his love for Salvestra. But then, soothing him with honeyed words, she began to pay him compliments and to coax him gently into following the advice of his guardians. And she played her cards so cleverly that in the end he agreed that he should go and stay there, but only for twelve months, and so it was arranged.

Still passionately in love, Girolamo went off to Paris, where he was detained by a series of delaying tactics for two whole years. On returning to Florence, more deeply in love than before, he was mortified to discover that his beloved Salvestra was married to a worthy young man who was by trade a tentmaker. Since there was nothing he could do about it, he tried to reconcile himself to the situation; and having inquired into where she was living, he began to walk up and down in the manner of a lovelorn youth outside her house, being convinced that she could not have forgotten him, any more than he had forgotten her. But this was not the case, for as the young man very soon perceived, to his no small sorrow, she no more remembered him than if she had never seen him before, and if she did indeed recollect anything at all, she certainly never showed it. Nevertheless the young man did everything he could to make her acknowledge him again; but feeling that he was getting nowhere, he resolved to speak to her in private, even if he were to die in the attempt.

Having inquired of a person living nearby regarding the disposition of the rooms, he secretly let himself in to the house one evening whilst she and her husband were attending a wake with some neighbours of theirs, and concealed himself behind some sheets of canvas that were stretched across a corner of her bedroom. There he waited until they had returned home and retired to bed, and when he was sure that her husband was asleep, he crept over to that part of the room where he had seen Salvestra lying down, placed his hand on her bosom, and said:

'Are you asleep already, my dearest?'

The girl, who was not asleep, was about to scream when the young man hastily added:

'For pity's sake, do not scream, for it is only your Girolamo.'

On hearing this, she trembled from head to toe, and said:

'Oh, merciful heavens, do go away Girolamo. We are no longer children, and the time has passed for proclaiming our love from the house-tops. As you can see, I am married, and therefore it is no longer proper for me to care for any other man but my husband. Hence I beseech you in God's name to get out of here. If my husband were to hear you, even supposing nothing more serious came of it, it would certainly follow that I could never live in peace with him again, whereas up to now he has loved me and we live calmly and contentedly together.'

To hear her talking like this, the young man was driven to the brink of despair. He reminded her of the times they had spent in each other's company and of the fact that his love for her had never diminished despite their separation. He poured out a stream of entreaties and promised her the moon. But he was unable to make the slightest impression.

All he wanted to do now was to die, and so finally, invoking the great love he bore her, he pleaded with her to let him lie down at her side so that he could get warm, pointing out that his limbs had turned numb with cold whilst he was waiting for her. He assured her that he would neither talk to her nor touch her, and promised to go away as soon as he had warmed himself up a little.

Feeling rather sorry for him, Salvestra agreed to let him do it, but only if he kept his promises. So the young man lay down at her side without attempting to touch her, and, concentrating his thoughts on his long love for her, on her present coldness towards him, and on the dashing of his hopes, he resolved not to go on living. Without uttering a word, he clenched his fists and held his breath until finally he expired at her side.

After a while, wondering what he was doing and fearing lest her husband should wake up, the girl made a move.

'Girolamo,' she whispered, 'it's time for you to be going.'

On receiving no answer, she assumed that he had fallen asleep. So she stretched out her hand to wake him up and began to prod him, but found to her great astonishment that he was as cold as ice to the touch. She then prodded him more vigorously but it had no effect, and after trying once more she realized that he was dead. The discovery filled her with dismay and for some time she lay there without the slightest notion what to do.

In the end she decided to put the case to her husband without saying who was involved, and ask his opinion about what the people concerned ought to do about it; and having woken him up, she described her own recent experience as though it had happened to someone else, then asked him what advice he would give supposing it had happened to her.

To this, the worthy soul replied that in his view, the fellow who was dead would have to be taken quietly back to his own house and left there, and that no resentment should be harboured against the woman, who did not appear to him to have done any wrong.

'In that case,' said the girl, 'we shall have to do likewise.' And taking his hand, she brought it into contact with the young man's body, whereupon he leapt to his feet in utter consternation, lighted a lamp, and, without entering into further discussion with his wife, dressed the body in its own clothes. And without further ado, he lifted it on to his shoulders and carried it, confident in his own innocence, to the door of Girolamo's house, where he put it down and left it.

Next morning, when the young man's corpse was discovered lying on the doorstep, a great commotion was raised, in particular by the mother. The body was carefully examined all over, but no trace of a wound or a blow could be found, and it was the general opinion of the physicians that he had died of grief, as indeed he had. His remains were taken into a church, to which the sorrowing mother came with numerous kinswomen and neighbours, and they all began to weep and keen over his body, as is customary in our part of the world.

Whilst the tears and lamentations were at their height, the worthy man in whose house Girolamo had died turned to Salvestra and said:

'Just cover your head in a mantle and go over to the church where Girolamo was taken. Mingle with the women, and listen to what they are saying about this business, and I will do the same among the men, so that we may find out whether anything is being said against us.'

The girl readily assented, for she was stirred to pity now it was too late and was eager to gaze upon the dead features of the man who had been unable to persuade her, whilst he was still alive, to grant him so much as a single kiss. And so off she went to the church.

What a wonderful thing Love is, and how difficult

it is to fathom its deep and powerful currents! The girl's heart, which had remained sealed to Girolamo for as long as he was smiled upon by Fortune, was unlocked by his far from fortunate death. The flames of her former love were rekindled, and no sooner did she catch sight of his dead face than they were all instantly transformed into so much compassion that she edged her way forward, wrapped in her mantle, through the cluster of women mourners, coming to a halt only when she was almost on top of the corpse itself. Then with a piercing scream, she flung herself upon the dead youth, and if she failed to drench his face with her tears, that was because, almost as soon as she touched him, she died, like the young man, from a surfeit of grief.

The women, who had thus far failed to recognize her, crowded round to console her and urge her to her feet, but since she did not respond they tried to lift her themselves, only to discover that she was quite still and rigid. And when they finally succeeded in raising her, they saw at one and the same time that it was Salvestra and that she was dead. The women now had double cause for weeping, and they all began wailing again much more loudly than before.

The news spread through the church to the men outside and reached the ears of her husband, who happened to be standing in their midst. Having burst into tears, he simply went on crying, oblivious to the efforts of various bystanders to console and comfort him; but eventually he told several of them about what had occurred the night before between this young man and his wife, thus clearing up the mystery of their deaths, and everyone was filled with enormous sorrow.

The dead girl was taken up and decked out in all the finery with which we are wont to adorn the bodies of the dead, then she was laid on the selfsame bier upon which the young man was already lying. For a long time they mourned her, and afterwards the two bodies were interred in a single tomb: and thus it was that those whom Love had failed to join together in life were inseparably linked to each other in death.

The Eaten Heart

You must know, then, that according to the Provençals, there once lived in Provence two noble knights, each of whom owned several castles and had a number of dependants. The name of the first was Guillaume de Roussillon, whilst the other was called Guillaume de Cabestanh. Since both men excelled in feats of daring, they were bosom friends and made a point of accompanying one another to jousts and tournaments and other armed contests, each bearing the same device.

Although the castles in which they lived were some ten miles apart, Guillaume de Cabestanh chanced to fall hopelessly in love with the charming and very beautiful wife of Guillaume de Roussillon, and, notwithstanding the bonds of friendship and brotherhood that united the two men, he managed in various subtle ways to bring his love to the lady's notice. The lady, knowing him to be a most gallant knight, was deeply flattered, and began to regard him with so much affection that there was nothing she loved or desired more deeply. All that remained for him to do was to approach her directly, which he very soon did, and from then on they met at frequent intervals for the purpose of making passionate love to one another.

One day, however, they were incautious enough to be espied by the lady's husband, who was so incensed by the spectacle that his great love for Cabestanh was transformed into mortal hatred. He firmly resolved to do away with him, but concealed his intentions far more successfully than the lovers had been able to conceal their love.

His mind being thus made up, Roussillon happened to hear of a great tournament that was to be held in France. He promptly sent word of it to Cabestanh and asked him whether he would care to call upon him, so that they could talk it over together and decide whether or not to go and how they were to get there. Cabestanh was delighted to hear of it, and sent back word to say that he would come and sup with him next day without fail.

On receiving Cabestanh's message, Roussillon judged this to be his opportunity for killing him. Next day, he armed himself, took horse with a few of his men, and lay in ambush about a mile away from his castle, in a wood through which Cabestanh was bound to pass. After a long wait, he saw him approaching, unarmed, and followed by two of his men, who were likewise unarmed, for he never suspected for a moment that he was running into danger. Roussillon waited until Cabestanh was at close range, then he rushed out at him with murder and destruction in his heart, brandishing a lance above his head and shouting: 'Traitor, you are dead!' And before the words were out of his mouth he had driven the lance through Cabestanh's breast.

Cabestanh was powerless to defend himself, or even to utter a word, and on being run through by the lance he fell to the ground. A moment later he was dead, and his men, without stopping to see who had perpetrated the deed, turned the heads of their horses and galloped away as fast as they could in the direction of their master's castle.

Dismounting from his horse, Roussillon cut open Cabestanh's chest with a knife, tore out the heart with his own hands, and, wrapping it up in a banderole, told one of his men to take it away. Having given strict orders that no one was to breathe a word about what had happened, he then remounted and rode back to his castle, by which time it was already dark.

The lady had heard that Cabestanh was to be there that evening for supper and was eagerly waiting for him to arrive. When she saw her husband arriving without him she was greatly surprised, and said to him:

'And how is it, my lord, that Cabestanh has not come?'

To which her husband replied:

'Madam, I have received word from him that he cannot be here until tomorrow.'

Roussillon left her standing there, feeling somewhat perturbed, and when he had dismounted, he summoned the cook and said to him:

'You are to take this boar's heart and see to it that you prepare the finest and most succulent dish you can devise. When I am seated at table, send it in to me in a silver tureen.'

The cook took the heart away, minced it, and added a goodly quantity of fine spices, employing all his skill and loving care and turning it into a dish that was too exquisite for words.

When it was time for dinner, Roussillon sat down at the table with his lady. Food was brought in, but he was unable to do more than nibble at it because his mind was dwelling upon the terrible deed he had committed. Then the cook sent in his special dish, which Roussillon told them to set before his lady, saying that he had no appetite that evening.

He remarked on how delicious it looked, and the lady, whose appetite was excellent, began to eat it, finding it so tasty a dish that she ate every scrap of it.

On observing that his lady had finished it down to the last morsel, the knight said:

'What did you think of that, madam?'

'In good faith, my lord,' replied the lady, 'I liked it very much.'

'So help me God,' exclaimed the knight, 'I do believe you did. But I am not surprised to find that you liked it dead, because when it was alive you liked it better than anything else in the whole world.'

On hearing this, the lady was silent for a while; then she said:

'How say you? What is this that you have caused me to eat?'

'That which you have eaten,' replied the knight, 'was in fact the heart of Guillaume de Cabestanh, with whom you, faithless woman that you are, were so infatuated. And you may rest assured that it was truly his, because I tore it from his breast myself, with these very hands, a little before I returned home.'

You can all imagine the anguish suffered by the lady on hearing such tidings of Cabestanh, whom she loved more dearly than anything else in the world. But after a while, she said:

'This can only have been the work of an evil and treacherous knight, for if, of my own free will, I abused you by making him the master of my love, it was not he but I that should have paid the penalty for it. But God forbid that any other food should pass my lips now that I have partaken of such excellent fare as the heart of so gallant and courteous a knight as Guillaume de Cabestanh.'

And rising to her feet, she retreated a few steps to an open window, through which without a second thought she allowed herself to fall.

The window was situated high above the ground, so that the lady was not only killed by her fall but almost completely disfigured.

The spectacle of his wife's fall threw Roussillon into a panic and made him repent the wickedness of his deed. And fearing the wrath of the local people and of the Count of Provence, he had his horses saddled and rode away.

By next morning the circumstances of the affair had become common knowledge throughout the whole of the district, and people were sent out from the castles of the lady's family and of Guillaume de Cabestanh to gather up the two bodies, which were later placed in a single tomb in the chapel of the lady's own castle amid widespread grief and mourning. And the tombstone bore an inscription, in verse, to indicate who was buried there and the manner and the cause of their deaths.

THE STORY OF PENGUIN CLASSICS

Before 1946 ...'Classics' are mainly the domain of academics and students, without readable editions for everyone else. This all changes when a little-known classicist, E. V. Rieu, presents Penguin founder Allen Lane with the translation of Homer's Odyssey that he has been working on and reading to his wife Nelly in his spare time.

1946 The Odyssey becomes the first Penguin Classic published, and promptly sells three million copies. Suddenly, classic books are no longer for the privileged few.

1950s Rieu, now series editor, turns to professional writers for the best modern, readable translations, including Dorothy L. Sayers's *Inferno* and Robert Graves's *The Twelve Caesars*, which revives the salacious original.

1960s 1961 sees the arrival of the Penguin Modern Classics, showcasing the best twentieth-century writers from around the world. Rieu retires in 1964, hailing the Penguin Classics list as 'the greatest educative force of the 20th century'.

1970s A new generation of translators arrives to swell the Penguin Classics ranks, and the list grows to encompass more philosophy, religion, science, history and politics.

1980s The Penguin American Library joins the Classics stable, with titles such as *The Last of the Mohicans* safeguarded. Penguin Classics now offers the most comprehensive library of world literature available.

1990s Penguin Popular Classics are launched, offering readers budget editions of the greatest works of literature. Penguin Audiobooks brings the classics to a listening audience for the first time, and in 1999 the launch of the Penguin Classics website takes them online to an ever larger global readership.

The 21st Century Penguin Classics are rejacketed for the first time in nearly twenty years. This world famous series now consists of more than 1,300 titles, making the widest range of the best books ever written available to millions – and constantly redefining the meaning of what makes a 'classic'.

The Odyssey continues ...

The best books ever written

PENGUIN 🐧 CLASSICS

SINCE 1946

Find out more at www.penguinclassics.com